GW00499683

AFTERWORD

STORIES

JEREMY BIBAUD

Published by Pequod Publishing.

ISBN (Hardcover): 978-1-7781356-1-3

ISBN (Paperback): 978-1-7781356-0-6

ISBN (eBook): 978-1-7781356-2-0

Library and Archives Canada Cataloguing in Publication data available upon request to the publisher.

CONTENTS

INTRODUCTION

I've never read a book twice. I can count on one hand the number of movies I've watched a second time. That usually surprises people, but it's true. It might be my infatuation with technology that contributes to this, where change is a daily, sometimes hourly, occurrence. There's no room to be precious over what has already been erased or replaced by a newer, better version. That sounds so cold and mechanical when I read it back to myself, but it's true for that industry, at least.

So it strikes me as odd that my first collection of short stories looks into the past and explores professions that no longer exist, jobs that have been erased or replaced by a newer, better version.

This theme drew me in with more than that though, just like there are more to the reasons many of us read books twice or watch the same movies over and over—nostalgia, of course.

You'd be safe in arguing that nostalgia is the root of most, if not all, stories. In Greek, the word roughly translates to *the pain from an old wound*. It's romantic, sentimental, comforting, warm, transportive, but it's also a reminder of loss and how temporary and fleeting our reality is.

Despite many of the jobs I've written about in this collection being repulsive, degrading, or outdated by today's standards, it was the accounts I read from the people who worked them that made me realize I was writing about someone else's good ol' days. Not in the sense that anyone today would think of these professions fondly, but in the sense that anything good prior to *the now* is often remembered fondly and anything bad is often misremembered or forgotten entirely.

What surprised me most, though, was the sense of dignity in the way people spoke about some of these professions. The attitude that there is nobility in suffering has always felt false to me and part of a construct that tricks us into feeling pride when we are knocked down, degraded and, eventually, deemed outdated by those in stations above us. It's another measure of control.

I had to recognize that while these characters are not real, the jobs they performed were, and that, hopefully, allowed me to approach them with a sense of empathy. Writing these characters was often quite sad, and it's probably what compelled me to try to change their lives in small and significant ways when I could by providing them opportunities their real-life counterparts would never have imagined or offering a more comedic outlook on their livelihood.

I wanted a man with an embarrassing skill that would have made him the subject of ridicule to feel equally placed alongside one of the greatest composers the world has ever known. I wanted a male-dominated field to be subject to the first woman to attempt it, while highlighting all the difficulty that comes with being the first to do anything. I wanted a man who led two lives to be given the chance to pick one of them and try his best to make peace with the one left behind. This is how I approached all twelve characters in this collection. I hope, despite the fact their professions make them interesting to us now, that I was able to succeed in creating people just as fascinating as their professions.

This is my version of nostalgia, if it can still be called that. It isn't a longing for the way things were, it's a longing for how they might have been. It's cheating, I suppose, and if I reflect on it for even a moment, I can see to the root of my aversion.

If we only revisit things the way we think they were, we never have to acknowledge the way they actually are.

And that's the actual pain of an old wound.

Jeremy Bibaud, 2022

DEATH MASK

An Archmime was a jester who imitated the manners, gestures, and speech of the deceased and walked behind the corpse at funeral processions, performing impressions of the dead as if they were still alive.

THE INKY FABRIC felt cool against the back of Francisco's hand. It drew into itself the only light in the cramped space, and its blackness was unchanged to his eye. It dipped between the spaces of his fingers before he squeezed them together, crushing the fibres with arthritic knuckles. A few tired pops met the silence of the room.

"Are you satisfied?" A small man, even older than Francisco, spoke from the corner.

"You've done well, Guilherme," Francisco said, almost too gentle for the tailor to hear.

Guilherme, leaning in, nodded and released a slight exhale, betraying his calm manner. "Then I am pleased. I know how important this is."

"You have met a significant occasion with a garment that befits it, Guilherme. Thank you." Francisco reached for the tailor's shoulder and squeezed it. "Do you remember the first robe you made for me?"

"It is embarrassing to think on now, Francisco."

"It was a fine piece, Guilherme. You only think it embarrassing because of the quality you achieve now. If you were to live a second lifetime, you would find even this robe a disgrace."

The tailor eyed the robe, indulged in a moment of admiration, and replied, "I think not. This is a perfect piece." The old man smiled.

Francisco chuckled. "I suppose true masters only require one lifetime." He sighed. "I'll miss this, Guilherme."

"As will I. Shall I send in the bereaved?"

"Give me a few moments to dress and then, yes, send them in one at a time."

Guilherme nodded and left the room.

Francisco was alone now. Dust swirled through the air around him like tiny moths propelled by Lisbon wind and sound. He looked to the high window punched into the brown stone wall near the ceiling. From the basement room he could see the ankles and shoes of men and women and children passing by as they walked the market along Campo Santa Clara. It started to rain and the feet, caught unprepared, scurried along, looking for shelter.

Francisco wrapped the dark robe around his body and it settled across his shoulders and fell across his chest, weightless. He turned and took two large strides from the tall mirror to the narrow table and took a seat in one of the two wooden chairs. The fabric stretched with his long steps and he relaxed into the cloth. He ran his smooth hands across the table to a mask, face-down, in the centre. He tugged at the loose fastening ribbon, bringing it within reach and, gripping its plaster edges, turned it over to face him.

The face of the dead stared up at him. The eyelids had not been closed during its making and a thin white valley like a crescent moon lay between the unshut lids. It unsettled him. He flipped the mask over and fit it to his face. It glided across his cheeks and his forehead and nose and mouth filled the mould. He tied the ribbon in a too-tight knot behind his head and donned his wide-brimmed, flat-top hat.

The death mask kept all light from his eyes; he would be blind during his performance. Anxiety rushed into him when he reached out for the table and touched nothing but air, but a quick adjustment had him find it again and pushed the worry from his mind.

There was a knock at the door.

Francisco cleared his throat. "Enter."

A young man poked his head in. "Senhor, it is Miguel."

Francisco waved him in and motioned to the empty chair.

Miguel took a seat. They listened to the rain for several moments. Then he shifted his position as if to ready himself and said, "My mother, my whole family, we're honoured that you will be at my father's funeral."

"Thank you, Miguel, but I will not forget that it is not my day. It is your father's." Francisco's voice cracked. "I am sorry. My voice has been hoarse for several days."

"I've only ever known one archmime, my father. I hear you are the very best."

"I am now also the very last," Francisco said with a warm smile he hoped came through the plaster of the mask.

They were silent again. The rain splashed onto the street above.

"Do you know how an archmime prepares for a funeral, Miguel?"

"Not really. I'm ashamed to say I didn't take an interest in my father's work."

"I will meet with you, your sister, and your mother, and you will each tell me the one thing about your father that you will never forget. And from those qualities I will perfect an impression of the man to perform at the head of the funeral procession from this spot, through the Feira da Ladra, to the Church of Sao Vicente of Fora, where the ceremony will take place."

Miguel swallowed hard. "Senhor, can I ask why you do this?"

"To remind all who attend of your father in the physical way that he no longer can. I am a final image for those who could not imprint one on their minds before he passed."

"No, sir, you misunderstand. I mean, why do you dedicate your life to this, impersonating the dead?"

Francisco ran his hand across the grain of the wood table. "I suppose I was never any good at anything else. Miguel, do you know how you would like your father to be remembered?"

Miguel nodded. "I do."

"Tell me."

"I don't know how you can do it."

"That is my worry, not yours. Tell me."

"When I was a child, my father and I would run through the narrow streets of Alfama. He would chase me like an animal and I would hide in every doorway and alcove I came across. It was for fun, but it scared me too. That mixture of excitement and fear, it is why I am a matador. It is why I do not fear having lost my father, because I will see him again and again in the arena. The crowds will cheer my name and they will applaud a thousand moments of my father rushing past me, searching and searching, but never finding me. It will be like in Alfama, always."

Francisco breathed in. "But you must kill the bull in the end."

"I do. And that is me letting go of my father. I will celebrate his life and remember his death every time I fight. It is a morbid thought to many, but I know death differently than most. I'm sorry if this is not appropriate."

"Miguel, it is a perfect memory. Watch for me in the square as I lead your father's procession. You will feel the secret streets of Alfama. You will see your father as you did a child again."

"Thank you, senhor. I will get my sister." Miguel stood, paused in front of the mirror, and left through the door he entered by.

There was a knock a few moments later and a small girl, twelve years old, her hair unkempt, wild, the ends of which arched out at odd angles like brown lightning, stepped inside. "May I enter?" she asked.

"Of course," Francisco waved her in and motioned to the chair opposite him the same way he had Miguel.

She took two large strides and jumped into the chair. She stared at him without speaking, without moving.

"Does the mask frighten you?" he asked.

She nodded, then followed it with a sound of agreement when she realised he could not see her.

"I apologise. I need you to see me as your father. It will help with my work," he said.

She didn't respond.

"Do you know why you're here, Babetta?"

"To tell you a story," she whispered.

Francisco nodded, trying to shake the menace from the mask for the young girl.

"I don't have a story. It's just something he said to me once."

"What was it, child?" Francisco asked before clearing his throat, his voice still gruff.

"He found me in my room crying once. I was sad because my brother was leaving. It was only for three days, but I thought he was going forever."

"What did your father do when he found you?"

"He sat on the floor beside me and asked me why I was crying. He said, 'Babetta, you cry because you are afraid of being alone. You cry because you are human and you love your brother and you love your family, but you are afraid that if Miguel can leave, then we might also leave.'"

Francisco moved his hand across the table again in a wiping motion, pushing invisible crumbs into place. "Was he right?" he asked.

"He was, but I was too young to understand him and he knew.

So he looked at me and he smiled and said, 'Babetta, I will tell you one secret that you must never repeat to anyone else but me.'" She sniffled and wiped her eyes.

Francisco reached into his chest pocket for a handkerchief before realising he was wearing the robe. "Babetta, it is all right. I will tell no one else. Only you will know the truth of what he said to you when you watch me."

He heard her breathe in, the air catching in her chest in brief staccato. She jumped from the chair and hurried to the door. Francisco heard it open, but she did not leave. "He told me, 'Babetta, you will always be my favourite. You will always be my favourite.' And I believed him and I have only ever repeated it to him."

Then she left Francisco.

The rain had stopped. The sounds of animals, cows, chickens, rattled their way into the small chamber.

Without a knock, the last visitor, the wife of the deceased, entered the room. Francisco stood. "Djanira, please," he motioned to the chair for a third time.

She sat down, her heavy dress brushed against the wood chair as she took her seat. "Archmime, you do my husband a great honour," she said.

"You do your husband greater honour, Djanira. Your children are thoughtful and...my tailor, he tells me you spend great effort in the markets. The merchants of Alfama respect you. I suspect you will not have trouble providing for your family."

"No, I will not, but a family does not live on coin alone."

"Of course not."

"Archmime, I must confess I don't recall my husband ever mentioning you. It surprised me to see your name in the letter he left us. He had no friends I was aware of."

Francisco placed his hand over his heart. "It surprised me, too. We had not spoken since we trained together. I must have made an impression for him to recall me so many years later."

"Yes, quite an impression." Djanira crossed her legs, and the dress rustled again. She tapped her foot in midair; her ankle clicked each time. "I have thought about this conversation for days and I still don't know how I would like you to honour my husband."

"Your children have both told me stories of a man I wish I had known. You may do the same or you may share another detail. How he walked, or spoke, a favourite turn of phrase, a particular movement, any detail that might help me bring him to life for you."

She chuckled.

"Why do you laugh, Djanira?"

"I will tell you, archmime, that he walked with the lightness of a man who was not married, spoke with the ease and naivety of a man who had no children, and the only phrases he turned were tired aphorisms. He spun his hands when he spoke, twisted them at the wrist and flitted his fingers in a most unbecoming way. That is a man I do not wish to see brought to life."

Francisco leaned back in his chair; the wood creaked beneath him. He tugged on his hat, ensuring its position.

"The man your children spoke of left me with quite a different impression."

"It was not fatherhood he failed at, but manhood."

Francisco coughed, but his voice remained raspy. "Is this failure what you would have me project?" he asked.

"No. I just needed someone to know." Djanira stood and took quiet steps towards the door. "My husband was a conflicted man, archmime. I grieved the loss of our marriage many years ago. Today, at last, I want him to feel uncomplicated for the first and only time. That is my gift to him. The only gift he might have ever used." She exhaled. "Perform well."

Then Francisco was alone again. He removed his hat and pushed the death mask up and let it rest in his thinning hair. Many feet crowded near the window above him. A slow, silent mob of black filled the square outside.

He stood and faced himself in the mirror again, adjusted his robe, relaxed his body, and breathed.

"The last archmime," he whispered, the hoarseness in his throat now gone.

By the time he left the room and ascended the stairs to the street, someone had already positioned the casket to begin the procession. Grey clouds threatened the drying streets and a cool wind slid through his robe.

Francisco pulled the death mask over his face and repositioned his hat. He took two long strides from the doorway and the crowd noticed his presence and parted for him. He was blind now, but he had walked this path a hundred times, a thousand times.

It was twenty-seven paces in a straight line to the front of the procession. They would not begin until he took his position. The air became still as he approached the head of the column. The quiet rolled through the crowd like a blanket suffocating fire. The exertion from the men lifting the heavy casket reached his ears as he approached. There was a brief and hollow scrape as it left the stone street.

He dropped his head, letting the death creep into his bones, fill the tiny spaces between his joints and beat against the tiny bones in his inner ear. When he raised his head again, he had transformed in the eyes of all around him. It was a subtle effect, but convincing. The body inhabiting the disguise was gone. Only the deceased remained.

He stretched his arms out wide and spun in wild circles, lunging towards the crowd. They recoiled, then laughed. He babbled gibberish and threw his hands out in a most unbecoming manner. Mourners turned to revellers as he ran circles around the procession. By the time he reached Feira da Ladra, the crowd had tightened, and he jumped into their arms and they pushed the blind fool back into the middle before he ran to the opposite side and did the same.

Francisco's performance enraptured the surrounding crowd

and they swelled around him. He danced across every stone; he touched every inch of the square and every struggling weed between the rocks knew his presence.

"Point me towards the family!" he shouted and one mourner gripped him by the shoulders and aimed him towards the mother and her two children. He knelt down on one knee and placed a hand on the dusty stone. He grunted as a wild boar and charged the trio.

With each step, he shifted away from the jester, from the fool, from the most unbecoming, to the exciting, to the loving, to the feared. The crowd cheered him on as he closed the gap between himself and Djanira, Babetta, and Miguel. He heard Miguel's laugh, deep and excited, followed by him clapping his hands together.

Francisco continued his rush towards Miguel, and at the last moment stood upright and spun towards Babetta. The black cape rolled outward from Francisco's body and stretched around the girl, hiding them both from the gaze of the mob. He reached out to her, and felt her sweet grip on the tips of his fingers. He held the pose until she released him. She laughed through her sobs.

Francisco spun and ran back to the centre of the square to prepare himself for the last act. He crossed back in front of the procession. The sky had blued, and the sun warmed his neck. Energy from the crowd filled him and he was, at last, uncomplicated.

In his ecstasy, he lost focus, and his foot caught an upturned stone and he fell forward in a whirl of black silk and pooled into a mass in front of the procession. His jaw connected with the stone first and the death mask snapped; its rough edge caught his lip and fresh blood pumped into his mouth and spilled to the street. He lay still.

The men carrying the casket did not see the fallen body in time and tripped over Francisco's arms and legs. With their balance broken, their grip faltered. The casket fell to the earth, and the impact split the wood. The lid fell open and from inside poured dozens of sizable stones. They struck the ground beside Francisco with a quake he felt from inside his own chest.

The carousing stopped as the crowd returned to their quiet. The remaining pallbearers let down the rear of the casket. It was all gasps and murmurs now. Francisco remained motionless, with half of his face pressed against the dirt beneath him.

"It's full of stones!" one shouted.

"Where's the body?" another asked.

The mob pushed closer and soon Francisco, ignored, saw dozens of feet stamping around him, voices clamouring to view the evidence with their own eyes.

It was then that Francisco, confident he had become irrelevant to them now, pushed himself up and with the one eye he could now see with, made his way to the shadows of a narrow Alfama passage.

He stayed there for a time and watched the crowd in secret. He saw Djanira staring at the surrounding din. She clutched Babetta to her side, whose face was expressionless. Miguel sat in the dusty street beside them. Wind whipped his hair around his stretched face.

"Goodbye," Francisco whispered.

A tiny figure approached from the end of the street. He pulled two horses behind him. The beasts made little noise, their hooves muffled by grass growing over stone.

Francisco approached the man, and the shadow slid from his face. "Guilherme. I was wondering if you might not make it."

"The horses were less than cooperative," Guilherme said.

The two men threw their arms around one another. Guilherme's head nestled under Francisco's chin.

The mob dispersed, the distraction of scandal now waning. "I see the procession did not go as planned?"

"I tripped near the end. They discovered my body was not in the casket."

Francisco mounted a horse, as did Guilherme. The two men

turned their backs to the thinning crowd. They nudged their horses forward, pushing them towards the very edge of Lisbon and beyond.

"Do you have any regrets?" Guilherme asked.

Francisco looked over his shoulder, then back ahead. "Only that I do not have two lifetimes."

CHANDLER

A Chandler was responsible for the storage of wax and production of candles in wealthy medieval households, staples for homes before electrical lighting.

THE VOICE OF GOD THUNDERED, "Welcome back to the 54th Primetime Emmy Awards! Once again, here's your host, Conan O'Brien!"

He was awake. He thought he had died, but he was awake. After several infant-like steps to the left, he realised that what he had mistaken for God's eternal glory was just a great orb of light. He rattled his knuckles against its casing and the metal gonged back at him. He didn't know what kind of light it was. There was no flame anywhere inside, and no wax dripped around its base. It was as if the light just was. He supposed it could have been *a* god, but not *the* God.

Just then, his stomach caught up to him in the year two thousand and two. It vaulted against the inside of his ribcage. He dashed towards a rack of clothes and, after parting the hanging garments, threw up in the shadows behind it. He wiped the vomit that had splashed back onto his face on the sleeve of his simple purple robe.

A sound like thunder erupted around him and there was a flash of commotion from between red drapes suspended from the ceiling across the room. He stepped in stockinged feet across the darkened space and gripped the velvet fabric in his trembling hands and peered into the opening.

There was a crowd of thousands watching the stage he was peeking out on. The men all wore the same black coat and white tunic and their hair glistened as much as their teeth. The women who accompanied them were just as polished and wore elegant gowns of many colours. He keyed in on one particular blonde in the front row. Her lips gleamed red and her bosom, barely contained, heaved under a tight, silvery-scaled dress. *A courtesan for every man? Perhaps this is heaven after all.*

"Who the fuck are you supposed to be?" a shrill voice blurted from behind him.

He decided there was no use in being clever now that someone had found him. He turned to face the voice. It was a short woman with a large plume of red hair that shook when she spoke. "Good day, miss. I am a chandler from—"

"You're one of the Chandlers? Why haven't you fucking been to costume yet? Your group is about to go on! Go, go, go!" she screamed as she pushed him further backstage with the tip of a small square mechanism that cast a blue glow onto her face. The future was so full of light.

He stumbled into an area where dozens of people were engrossed in all manner of arcane tasks.

"Phil! I found one of your Chandlers snoopin' around the fucking curtain, Phil! Get a handle on your fucking Chandlers, Phil. Fuck you, Phil. Don't roll your fucking eyes at me! You're a piece of shit, Phil. An actual piece of shit. Ah, fuck you."

The red-haired woman screamed profanity with an ease that startled him. "Miss, there's no need–" he started.

"What the fuck are you still talking to me for? Move, Chandler."

A man with a bald head and ill-fitting black tunic, presumably named Phil, grabbed him by the elbow and pulled him towards a group of men all wearing the same dark pants, crisp white tunic with a sleeveless vest adorned with a pattern that made him dizzy. They swooped their hair to the side.

"What are you wearing?" Phil barked at him.

"As I tried to explain, I am a chandler from—"

"No, you're not a Chandler. You see these men?" Phil motioned to the group of mirror images. "These are Chandlers. In costume and ready to go on stage to perform their skit in 90 seconds."

Phil's words stung and reignited the wound that had sent him here.

"The future does not need you, chandler."

His eyes flickered open and the long, silvery beard of the castle's art instructor and part-time mystic tickled his ear with every word whispered into it.

"Mystic Michael? What are you doing in my bedchamber?" he asked, pulling his wolf-skin blankets up to his chin.

"I had a vision," the ancient sage licked his lips, "of a bleak future in which chandlers and their revered expertise in candle making would be no longer. Mankind will enslave light and summon it whenever they desire as gods!"

The art instructor and part-time mystic was prone to dramatics, but the words haunted him for three days before he had asked the lunatic for help. "Wizard, tell me–"

"I am not a wizard. I am an art instructor and a mystic and a grief counsellor."

"Grief counsellor? When did this happen?"

"Forthwith."

"Forthwith?"

"The King hath decreed that I will forthwith be the castle's grief counsellor. He hath said it, let it be so."

The chandler breathed in. "Art instructor, part-time mystic, and grief counsellor, tell me, are your words true? Is my life's work a waste?"

"Of course. Acrylics and prediction are my specialties. Do not take me for a conjurer of cheap tricks! If you need a potion to make your tomato plant bloom, see Merle."

The chandler asked, "Can I see the future?"

The art instructor, part-time mystic, and newly appointed part-time grief counsellor scrunched his mouth to the side and thought for a moment, "I have a portrait to paint tomorrow afternoon..."

"Whose portrait?"

"The Prince."

"The King has no heir."

"He is in utero at present, but you didn't hear it from Mystic Michael."

"I wish I hadn't. Can you help me in the morning?"

"I suppose I could brew you a..."

"Potion?"

"Elixir! I could brew you an elixir to transport you to the moment your kind will fall."

The chandler thought about this. "If what you say is true—"

"It is."

"...and there is no way to stop these events, do not show me the moment my dedication to this craft will feel the most futile. Search the phantasms that wander your touched mind for a time in which my kind is most popular. Show me a day in which the world knows our name and the light of candles brings a smile to the lips of adult and babe alike. If I cannot find some hope for my vocation at that moment, then I will at least take solace in being surrounded by my brethren at our peak."

"Sure."

"I need your help, Susan!"

"Phil, you piece of shit. I am trying to find club soda! Ray fucking Romano spilled marinara sauce on his shirt and he's on stage in 45 seconds. Where the fuck do you get marinara sauce at the Prime fucking Time Emmy Awards, Phil? You tell me that and I'll not only dress your fucking Chandler, I'll throw in a blowie!"

"They're serving mozza sticks with marin—"

"Fuck you, Phil!"

The red-haired lady, Susan, was undressing him when his mind snapped back into the year two thousand and two. Had he regained his wits in time, modesty would have dictated he protest.

In less than twenty seconds, he found himself dressed like the other men huddled together before him. They all stared back, mouths agape.

"Fuck me, you look just like him," Susan gasped.

"Like who?"

"Oh, fuck you. Where do you find these fucks, Phil?"

Phil shrugged. "Okay everyone, we're on right after commercial. Link arms now. Lead Chandler," Phil pointed at the chandler closest to the curtain, "Wait for your cue. It should come in 10...9...8..."

This is it. Mystic Michael did his job well.

He was arm-in-arm with a dozen other chandlers.

Is this the last of my kind? A final celebration of our craft before mankind ascends to the realm of gods?

"7...6...5..."

"Matthew, what are you doing back here? I thought you were just going to the washroom," a soft, feminine voice cooed.

He looked to his right, and awe replaced his newfound camaraderie. The woman who stood next to him, her delicate tanned hand resting on his arm like a flower rests its petal on a dew drop, shone like the sun. Her black dress was modest, but clung to her body like liquid. She bared sun-kissed shoulders and their caramel colour matched her hair. She smiled at him, dazzling and white. He melted like wax under her heat.

"Matthew! I won!" she screamed and shoved a shining figure into his face. A winged woman stripped of clothing, supporting a glowing ball of gold.

Was this it? Was this the device that had captured the light and ruined his kind?

"What are you doing here? Come on, we have to get back to our seats. They're doing Comedy Series next and I have a good feeling this year."

"It's been eight years, Jen. I think if we were going to win, we would have by now, " said another man who had just approached.

Jen slapped him across his arm. "Oh, stop it, David. We'll get it this time. Let's get back to our seats."

He unlinked from his fellow chandlers, drawn to the lavender scent wafting from Jen's hair. *Jen. Jen.* Even her name was exotic to him.

Then she let go of his arm and drifted away to a sea of flashing light.

"Buddy, are you doing a skit tonight? Why are you dressed like Chandler?" David laughed. "Where's your tux?"

"I, I don't know, David. They took my clothes."

"Okay, look, I don't know if this is something your agent told you to do or what, but if we win, you're going to thank me for this."

David pulled him back into the darkened area he had woken up in and began sorting through the clothes the chandler had thrown up behind.

"Smells like vomit over here."

"It does. And that is still a disgusting thing, right?" the chandler asked.

"Uh, yeah, Matthew. It is still a disgusting thing. What is up with you? Here, this should fit."

He took the clothes from David and changed into them. Now he and David matched.

"All right. Better. Let's get back. Good vibes, buddy. Good vibes."

He followed David back to his seat. He was amongst the glossy hair and teeth now. Bosoms rose and fell, overwhelming him with the light they seemed to hold within them.

"No, you're over there," David said, pointing to a vacant spot a few seats over.

"Ladies and gentlemen, Jay Leno," the voice of God said.

A distinguished, grey-haired man walked across the stage and spoke. The chandler tried to pay attention to his words, but he couldn't focus; his mind was swimming. He had seen enough and could feel himself on the verge of tears. Knowing that not a single ray of the warmth covering this crowd came from a candle was too much for him to bear.

I must steal the device and bring it back to Mystic Michael. He will be able to stop it.

He spied another lovely young beauty on the edge of the stage, holding the device that Jen had held in her hands earlier. Living pictures on the stage depicted the golden idol as if it was to be worshipped. It must be the key.

I will run to the stage and snatch the trinket from that pretty courtesan's hands and hide until the time elixir wears off. He was sweating through the fine clothes he wore. *I can do this.* He gripped the arms of his chair. His fingers sunk into the soft material.

"Hey, you can see through these envelopes," the man on stage mused.

The audience laughed. *They will not be laughing for long.*

"The winner is...Friends."

He jumped from his seat and, to his surprise, so did everyone around him. The crowd roared. *Can they read my thoughts?* He fell in with a group of white teeth and shiny hair and beautiful, coloured gowns and floated along down the aisle to the stage and up the stairs and onto the shiny floor and the heaving bosom passed the device to another gentleman a mere arm's length from him.

This was the moment. *I have nothing to fear now.* He would lunge for the device and run backstage, where he would find a shadow to crawl into. *On the count of three.*

1...2...

The group moved backstage. A tall, red-haired man walked out in front of them and waved to the audience.

Even better. I will make my move where no one will witness it. He shuffled his way closer to the man who clutched the brilliant doom in his hands.

"Matthew! Hold this for me, will you?"

Their hubris has blinded them. In his excitement, the fool is handing the key to the one person present who would steal it from him.

The chandler reached out for the statue, but the man moved past him to someone else. He turned and saw the intended target. It was...him. The one called Matthew. He was the spitting image of himself.

Matthew noticed the chandler staring at him. "Whoa, these seat fillers are getting scary good. Could this guy *be* any more my twin?" he asked.

The group did a double-take, burst into a fit of laughter, then, too, joined the sea of flashing light that had consumed Jen earlier.

The chandler was alone now. Failure closed in around him like a thick sheet. He mouthed his thoughts in whispers only he could hear, "Why did I focus on candlemaking alone? Why didn't I become a triple threat like Mystic Michael? I have been shortsighted. There is no hope for my kind. The future has no need of me."

Then he was back in the castle, the effects of the elixir having worn off. The last of his bedside candles flickered against the suffocating darkness. He leaned over and blew it out.

Executive Producers
Kevin S. Bright
Marta Kauffman
David Crane

BLUE BIRD

A familiar site in 18th century Edinburgh neighbourhoods was the Wha' Wants Me? Man, a gentleman who carried a portable toilet and a small curtain for your privacy that he could loan you for a small fee.

"The first time Wendy Chapman pulled a bucket out from under a stranger's arse, she almost added the contents of her stomach to the coiled mass she held in her hands..."

"Excuse me?" Wendy asked.

"I'm writing a story about you. For the *Edinburgh Courant*. I'm the editor there. My name is Geoffrey," he said, gesturing as if greeting royalty.

"I don't want a story about me in the *Courant*, Geoffrey."

"It's no trouble. I pick the stories that appear. I'm the editor."

"Yes, I heard you. I still don't want a story about me in the *Courant*."

"Well, what do you want?" he asked, a look of confusion creasing his forehead.

"What do *you* want?" she returned.

"I want to buy you dinner."

"Do you have to be there when I eat it?" Wendy asked.

"Preferably."

"Then no, I don't want dinner either. Are you done down there?" Wendy asked. She opened the privacy robe. "There are other customers."

"I actually didn't have to go. I just wanted to speak with you."

"You're still paying me."

"Of course, of course," he paused, "Would you take payment in the form of a free dinner?"

"No. I take payment in coin."

Dejected, the editor of the *Edinburgh Courant* stood from the box wherein hundreds of others had emptied their bowels before him. Wendy pulled her arms back from around the man and so brought back the privacy robe with them. The man placed two coins on the edge of the box and strolled away from her. His shoes, brown with mud, sloshed through the sloppy streets of Edinburgh's Old Town.

Wendy watched the man leave until a Highland cow stomping through the market cut her gaze off, its tawny hair swaying in front of its eyes as it lumbered through the muck. Wendy picked the box up and followed it.

"Wha-wants-me!" she shouted. "Wha-wants-me!"

No takers from the thin morning crowd of men who hadn't yet found their home after a night of drinking.

"Aye! Gimme dat shit box, lassie!" a grating voice hollered.

She turned and the look of annoyance on her face dissolved into one of being mildly perturbed.

"Max, no one says that to me!"

"Seriously? That's the only way I *would* ask. Which I wouldn't, for the record."

"That's a relief. I think that might cross the line of our professional relationship."

"Is that all we are, Wendy? A professional relationship?" he asked, smirking.

She pushed him to the side. "You finish my new robe yet? After three washes, this one still stinks.

"What does it stink like?"

"Heather, Max. It stinks like heather and honey. That's why I need a new one, because I need it to smell more like shit and less like flowers."

"Sarcasm is not an attractive trait, Wendy. In fact, it might even hurt business. Do you speak this way to your customers?"

"I'll have you know my customers adore me."

"So I've heard..."

"What have you heard?"

"I hear men from New Town muddy their silk slippers in Old Town just to find the world's first female Wha-Wants-Me Man. They're all smitten by your beauty and entrepreneurial spirit."

"Entrepreneurial? Max, have you been reading again? You know you won't find a wife using words like that."

"I met a girl last week."

"I met you today. Doesn't mean anything."

"Doesn't it, though?"

Wendy jumped onto a nearby crate, her robe snagging on the loose slivers of the unsanded box.

"I thought this would be different. I knew it wouldn't be easy, but I thought the hard part would be stinking like shit. It turns out shit is only sickening the first few times."

Max jumped onto the crate with Wendy.

"The hard part is knowing that every man who calls me over is going to, at some point, every time, turn to me while taking a shit and cock his head like he's just now noticed me, despite having watched me like a creep for a good ten minutes beforehand, and say, 'Oh, lass. You're a pretty one, ain't ya? Would ya fancy a roll in the hay after this?'"

"You seem to attract a very specific clientele."

"I guess they think I don't mind getting dirty and that must mean I'm also a woman of loose morals."

"And that isn't true!" Max said, without conviction. "I mean, it's not, right? I don't want to assume."

"Why can't they just treat me like the butcher, the fishmonger, even the barman? Make use of my services in silence and, if you must talk, confess your sins like a good drunk and move along."

Max put his arm around her shoulders. "Eventually, you'll have rejected the whole of Edinburgh and you won't have to worry about this anymore."

"You're such a shit sometimes." She shrugged his arm off from around her shoulders.

"Would a shit have stayed up all night making you this?" He pulled his bag to his front and reached inside it. He whipped out a shimmering black robe, and the fabric rustled across her lap.

"It's cotton. It took a while to stain and perfume, but it should hold up against odour."

Wendy sunk her hands into the thin fabric and her fingers disappeared in its folds.

"Are you serious, Max? You already finished the robe! It's perfect!"

She leaped from the box.

"Don't look!" She reached her hand out to Max as if to block his view.

"I made you a robe. You're a fool if you think I'm not going to look."

She glanced down the street to see if anyone was watching and, when they were alone, whipped off the musty robe she was wearing and wriggled into the new one.

"This is brilliant, Max. It covers me even better than the old one and the privacy cloth is longer, so I won't have to stretch my arms so far anymore. I almost fell onto a gentleman's lap this morning. That wouldn't have helped my case any."

Wendy spun in the robe and for a moment her pale skin

vanished in the cloth and she appeared like laundry on a line, tossed by Scottish winds. She stopped spinning and brought the cloth up to her face and inhaled.

"Is that...heather?"

"It is. Lucky guess." Max smiled. "I need to get back."

Wendy draped herself in the cloth. "Max, it will more than do. I'm not sure I'll be able to repay you."

"I know."

"Well, maybe someday."

"Right, well, I have to get back to work. I'm glad you like it." Max nodded at Wendy, and wandered off down the street with a slight skip in his step.

Wendy floated back down the streets she had just walked. The walls on either side of her were brighter, a blue door was deeper in hue, a pig, somehow even more happy to be covered in mud than before. The robe felt cool against her forearms and it fluttered in the breeze. A horse and carriage rushed by and splashed a murky puddle up and toward her, but she sidestepped the wave of sludge and carried on into the Grassmarket again.

"Wha-wants-me!" she shouted, lifting the box over her head, waving it around until her arms grew tired.

No takers.

Wendy walked to the far side of the market, weaving through the thickening crowd of merchants and cows and merchants who reeked like cows. A fish flew through the air so close to her face the aroma of the sea lingered in her nostrils. The sun lit its scales like a wet, rainbow scarf and it drew her eyes along its path, which was unfortunate, as it did not prepare her for the second fish that smacked into her and curled around her face. Slime and salt filled her mouth before she stumbled and fell to her knees.

A fishmonger shouted his apologies. She stood, nodded and smiled, impervious to whatever this day could throw at her.

"Wha-wants-me!" she shouted, her arms held high above her, a toothy smile across her face, a small bit of seaweed stuck in her red hair.

"I want you, lass. I want you to wrap your hands around me bawsack!" a phlegm-riddled voice lobbied from the crowd. A few people around her giggled.

Wendy sighed and went home.

The next several days were busy. Business seemed to pick up and, like Max had warned, she was seeing several customers from New Town trudging into Old Town to see the first female Wha-Wants-Me Man. Their clothes were finer, and they were well-mannered, but their shit stank the same.

At first, Wendy appreciated having a clientele that didn't propose to her or inundate her with invitations to dinner but, under the curious eyes of this set, she quickly felt like an animal in a zoo. It was still preferable, though.

By midday, her regular customers returned.

"Y'know, lass, it seems only right seeing as you've seen me arse, that ye show me yours," a young man said to her, his teeth as brown as the excrement he had passed.

"I haven't seen your arse, but if it's anything like your wee pecker, then I'll pass. Leave your money. Move along."

The afternoon passed into evening and the editor of the *Edinburgh Courant* returned.

"Okay, no dinner, just an ale...or a tea, and you let me interview you for my article."

"No."

"What kind of woman says no to tea?"

"A working woman, Geoffrey. I'm working. Right now. You shitting. Me, using this ample robe to give you some privacy. That's my work. I provide a service. So finish up so I can find more customers who will propose to me."

"Fine. You leave me no choice, Wendy. I will publish my article in tomorrow's paper with or without your interview. Then, when your business increases tenfold, you will know who to thank, but I may not be so willing to go to tea with you then."

"Well, why would I want to? You would have already increased my business. You can't offer me anything else."

"Gratit— you're a nasty woman, Wendy Chapman. A nasty woman."

Geoffrey handed her a coin and stomped away.

"How would you like them to treat you? I hate to break it to you, but you haul shit around. That kind of profession ranks pretty low in prestige," Max said, a mouthful of steaming beef pie half-chewed in his mouth.

"I suppose it *is* just slightly more prestigious than a tailor. Tell me, Max, how do you deal with everyone's disrespect?" she asked, her face earnest.

"I don't have to take this abuse. I'm already dining with someone beneath my station. Good day."

"Easy, easy. I didn't know you were so sensitive, Max. No more teasing," Wendy said, dragging her fork through the soft peas and carrots in her pie. "You know what it is, Max? It's that I treat all of my customers with dignity and they refuse to return it. There they are, in the middle of the busiest square in Old Town with their pants around their ankles, the previous day's dinner hanging out their arse, and I'm there shielding them from humiliation, averting my eyes to give them as much privacy and respect as one can in that situation, and they repay this kindness by telling me I have nice tits. The other workers don't hear squat from their customers. They don't even believe me when I tell them the stories."

"I suppose this is your reward for blazing a trail. Well, technically, your reward is their money. You're getting a lot more business than the other men now. It's a shame people don't know that."

Wendy dropped her fork and bits of pie crust flew into Max's face.

"Hey!"

"That's it! Max, that's it. I'll raise my prices."

"What?"

"You're right. Men want to talk to me. I'll raise my prices and make them earn it. Then, they'll think twice about throwing their time away because they've paid extra for it."

"I...don't...think, no, actually, maybe?" Max mumbled.

"Max, can you convince your boss to clean my robe each week?"

"Each week? For free?"

"At first, but I'll be able to pay for it eventually. Tell him to consider it an investment."

"I'll ask, but he isn't the charitable type."

"Thank you," Wendy said, beaming as she rushed from the shop.

That evening, Wendy attached wide strips of leather around the hole in her box, nailed it down at the edges, and filled it with sheep's wool. She gave it a sit. It was different, but better.

The next morning Wendy walked into Edinburgh's Grassmarket with a price quadruple that of her closest competitor. The other workers laughed at her.

She began with her usual invitation, shouting through the empty square. The morning was slow. The night's leftover drunks were not willing to pay such a premium to use her facilities.

Max walked into the square and rushed over to her. "My boss agreed to it!"

"What? For free?"

"Pretty much, yeah!"

"Max, what does *pretty much* mean?"

"Nothing, I'm just going to work an extra shift until you're able to pay for it yourself."

"Max..." Her small body relaxed under the large robe and then she jumped at him, wrapping her arms around his neck.

"Okay, okay, it's not that big a deal. You'll be paying for it yourself in no time."

"Max, you're the sweetest. Thank you." She held his hand, hidden under the folds of her robe.

Max cleared his throat. "How's business so far?"

Wendy smiled, "About to get a lot busier."

"Yeah?"

"Yeah."

Wendy spun around and climbed on top of a nearby crate.

The market was filling up with merchants selling fresh produce, fish, and poultry, and customers, eager to get first pick, were lining up at the stalls.

Wendy brought her hands to her mouth and began shouting, "Ladies and gentleman of Old Town, thank you for your attention. My name is Wendy Chapman and many of you know I am Edinburgh's, nay, the world's first and only female Wha-wants-me Man."

A few heads in the crowd turned.

Wendy continued, "For months I have served you, humbly and discreetly assisting you with a private and respectful space to relieve yourself en route to your destinations. I am here this morning to offer you an option unmatched by my peers."

She wobbled on the unsteady crate and Max moved in to hold it steady.

"I will afford you the same privacy you expect from me, but you will also have the most comfortable and pleasing experience as well. Your arse is my business! Your arse deserves better than hard wood and splinters. Your arse should be cushioned by the most luxurious wool. Your arse should be pressed against the softest of leathers. And you should be able to take a shit without smelling the previous dozen customers while you do it!"

Wendy looked down at Max and winked. A murmur spread through the market as people noticed the girl yelling on the crate.

"Your arse deserves better! You deserve better! Don't get your arse chapped, come to Chapman's Loo and experience the difference a woman's touch makes," Wendy shouted, holding her leather-cushioned loo above her head.

The crowd pointed at the revised box and went over to see what all the fuss was about. By noon, a line of customers stretched from the Grassmarket all the way to the Royal Mile. The line remained steady throughout the day, with customers wanting to test the Chapman difference.

Some still balked at the cost and told her she was mad for charging so much, but most were too curious not to give the girl a chance. They left satisfied, raving to their friends about the cushioned seat and the heather-scented privacy robe.

There were still a few who asked her to dinner, but the proximity and eagerness of other customers encouraged them to move along.

By the end of the first day, she had served more customers than in the previous two weeks combined. Her body ached and her back was sore from standing for so long, but she left the square satisfied for the first time since she started.

Wendy returned home and put a pot of water on her stove to heat for a bath. Her soiled robe, smelling less of heather and more like her business, she hung outside on a line to air out. She entered the outhouse a short distance from her home and rolled down her grey, knitted stockings into small bunches and placed them to the side. She hiked up her shift and sat down on the opening. Her muscles relaxed for the first time all day, and she let out an audible sigh of relief.

She took a deep breath and stared at a thick, white cobweb in the outhouse's corner until her eyes went fuzzy. She could have fallen asleep like this. Then a knock on the outhouse roused her.

She stiffened, remaining still and quiet. She wasn't expecting anyone. There was a soft knock again.

"...Yes?" she said.

No response.

"Hello? Who's there?"

"It's...Max."

"Max? What the hell are you knocking on my outhouse for?"

"I...wanted to ask you a question."

"Well, can it wait? I'm a little busy."

"No, I wanted to ask you now because, well, I thought it might be poetic, or something, if I asked you to dinner while you were...in the outhouse."

"Poetic?"

"Everyone always asks you to dinner while they're on your loo, so I thought it'd mean something if someone finally asked you while you were on the loo."

They were both silent for a period in which Wendy could have sworn the cobweb above her grew larger. Her pot of water whistled from inside her home.

She stood up, flattened her shift against her legs, and unlatched the door. It popped open, letting a bit of outside light and air in.

"Max, are you serious?"

"I am."

She laughed, as much to cover the awkwardness of the situation as to hide her disappointment.

THIS STORY IS NOT ABOUT YOU

An Arkwright designed chests, boxes, and coffers.

When you stand by the river outside your home, when the sun scatters itself across the water's surface and reveals its silver scales, your mind goes to his grey arms hanging limp down the sides of the final chest he ever crafted. With his passing, the gold inlay on the polished trunk corners was left incomplete. You finished it for him before you moved your mentor's body. It was difficult to work around him, but necessary. The chest held his heart, as is custom with all arkwrights.

He taught you the body is a series of chests stacked on top of one another. The feet are chests containing 26 bones each. The hands are similar, but with 27. The head, another chest, houses your mind. The body's trunk, never to be called a chest lest you confuse an arkwright, encases your organs. We never consider the heart as part of the trunk. It is a chest within a trunk. These are the lessons that flood back to you as you stand at the workshop table and stare down in silence at your own creation.

The lid is rounded and stained a rich, dark brown that appears as coal in the dim light of this space. You fashioned trunk corners similar to your mentor's. The candle flames dance yellow across the patterns grooved into the metal and splash onto tiny emeralds embedded into the very grain of the wood. It is otherworldly. A fitting home for the heart of an arkwright.

But you are not yet thirty years old and this will not be your last chest. You seek not the next life, but a brief repose from feeling the current one.

So here you are, standing above its curved lid, with a thin blade stuck between your ribs, blood pouring from the incision, you flip open the chest with your free hand and the blood pools in its base. Your arms tingle. You remove the blade with a quaking hand and set it on the table beside the box. You pull the skin on your trunk to the side and reach inside yourself, searching for your heart. Organs and muscle mush against one another as you push them to the side. Bone blocks your progress. You reach too far in and your fingertips slide across slick spine. It straightens at your touch. Your heart is further up. It beats against your forearm so you adjust your position until your trembling hand coils around it. You pull it out.

It scares you to look, so you close your eyes and lay it to rest on the floor of the chest. It smacks as it falls onto its side in the shallow pool of blood collecting at the bottom. You close the lid, then the wound.

You leave your workshop and walk the dusty path along the idle river. The sky, pink and yellow earlier, now appears a dismal grey. You push the door to your home open, not wishing to disturb your family. You take a deep breath in and it releases in small, short bursts. Your lungs stretch out to fill the hole where your heart was and the extra room allows them to swing inside of you like laundry on a line at every exhale.

You enter your room. Your wife is asleep. You step to the closet and pull out the suit jacket, pants, shirt, and tie you planned to wear to the wedding. The outfit seems drab to you now. You dress and go to the kitchen to prepare breakfast and discover your children have already started breakfast.

Your wound spots your white shirt with red dots so you button your jacket.

From the front door, your wife enters. You didn't even see her leave. She smiles and tells you she left for a morning walk while you were making breakfast. She says you look handsome, but doesn't join you, and instead leaves to dress for the wedding.

You walk to the church together. She holds your hand. Your son gets a grass stain on his only pair of nice pants. Your daughter eats a bug. These things do not bother you. You find an open pew near the middle of the church and sit down. The other guests arrive. They mingle, they laugh. You don't.

Men in tuxedos approach the front of the church. They take their appointed spots beside a priest. Women in unflattering dresses do the same. The bride enters. You dated once, four years ago. You wanted children; she didn't. She marches by. Her eyes linger on yours. She continues. They are married. They kiss. You watch dust swirl through a red beam of light cast from a high stained glass window, not because it's beautiful, but because it's the only thing moving. The ceremony ends. You leave.

Your wife heads inside your home to prepare lunch. You walk to your workshop. You are not afraid anymore. You aren't anything anymore. You open the lid to your chest.

There are two hearts where there should only be one.

The second one is smaller. You wrap steady fingers around the larger of the two and, spreading your wound open again, reinstate the heart in its proper position.

Your lungs cease their fluttering and with each breath, you start to feel again. Colour returns, along with fear and heartache. Emotion grips you with a baby's grasp, unexpected and surprising. You press down on the lid as if the unknown heart might spring forth like a jack-in-the-box.

Whose heart is this?

Your mind wanders back. You see her eyes again as they pass. You taught her your craft when you were together.

You close the door to your workshop. You lock it even. You stand by the river, its depths three shades of blue and full of life. Trout leap from it; a whitetail drinks from its cool surface. The sun warms your face. You think of her and imagine expressing thoughts buried so deep dust will gather on your lips.

You walk the trail back to your home. Your step is lighter. You enter the kitchen where your wife, still in the formal clothes she wore to the wedding, looking grayer by the day, by the hour, even, has prepared soup and sandwiches. Your children eat greedily and do not note your presence.

You decide then, between bites of a ham sandwich, to leave them.

The bread is fresh and sweetened with honey. The meat is a bright pink and the cheddar cheese satisfyingly sticks to the roof of your mouth. You wash it all down with a large glass of milk.

Your wife joins you at the table, her white blouse spotted with red dots of tomato soup.

HEPPIRI OTOKO

A Flatulist was an entertainer whose routine consists of passing gas in a creative and musical manner.

BEETHOVEN RAISED his fingers from the piano, stuck his right index finger into his ear, and wiggled it furiously. He then removed it and wiped it on his breeches.

"It's beautiful, Ludwig. Yet another masterpiece, to be sure," Gerhard said, suspending a small saucer and cup of tea over his crossed legs. He lifted the drink to his lips and slurped the too-hot water. "Do you remember the pieces you used to write? Their romance, their briskness," he paused, "I miss them," he said aloud, knowing the deaf composer would not hear.

Beethoven cleared his throat and said, "It will be Sonata Number 32."

"It's exquisite," Gerhard said. Gerhard walked to the piano and, pulling a notebook close to him, wrote, *It's beautiful, but abstract. What does it mean?*

Beethoven, as if only now realising Gerhard was even in the

room, snapped his head to the side to face the young man. His wild hair shook like ash lightning as he spoke. "When I came to Vienna, Mozart had just passed away. Everyone believed I would replace him and so I felt compelled to take on his flavour, and I believe I surrendered a bit of myself. Had I known the potential that lay within me...Well, this is me catching up."

Gerhard wrote again, *The music you've made is yours.*

Beethoven waved his fingers as if to shoo the words from the page. "Never mind that, I tell you this because when I lost my hearing, it delayed my development. But I've gained a second chance. If it wasn't for the good fortune of meeting the Heppiri Otoko, I may very well have never composed again."

Gerhard wrinkled his forehead in response to the exotic words.

"Have I never told you about the man who came from that faraway island seven years ago to help me hear again?" Beethoven asked, his lips twitching as if trying to move from a frown to a smirk.

A slice of golden light cut its way through the thick drapery hung in Beethoven's room. The leaves of the black poplar outside his bedroom window scattered the light from time to time as its branches shivered in the breeze.

The silk sheets of his bed were cool against his face. His quilt had knotted itself around his body during the night. He ran a finger along its stitching and picked at the tight threads with his fingernail.

The smell of earl grey tea met his nose. He breathed in, filled his lungs with bergamot, and held it for a few seconds before releasing the citrus scent into the air above him.

Reaching across to the end table, he pulled the tea towards him and blew into the steaming water. The surface rippled away from him, small waves crashing into porcelain cliffs. He sipped the drink too fast, and it burned his tongue and throat as he swallowed. He dropped the cup.

When it hit the floor, the ceramic shattered. Its shards spread out across the wood, tiny chips lost under rugs and ceramic dust under his bed.

All of this in silence

The tea itself was inconsequential. It wouldn't have made much noise, anyway.

Beethoven rolled back into his bed. He stayed there until the light left his room, the ticking of the grandfather clock in the hallway going ever unheard.

A month later Beethoven was, once again, sitting at his piano. He had been for a few days, pressing his fingers into the keys with such force his fingers ached, as if he was only now playing for the first time. He tried low notes, high notes, all the notes, but the sound no longer reached him.

His friends had stopped coming by. He saw shock and pity in their eyes and the effort to entertain them and their prayers for a miracle grated on him. They did not understand his mania, his desperation. They did not understand his solution.

Three days earlier, he had slammed his fist onto the keys and he felt the sound. It was inexplicable. It wracked his body as if he were the string being struck by the hammer. The sensation caused him to stand up straight. He laughed, but was soon disappointed by his inability to reproduce the effect.

It had been a phantom. A lingering tease his mind had saved to torture him. There would be no music for him.

A few weeks later, after a quick check-in from a much younger Gerhard and his father, Stephan, a guest arrived. Stephan placed an open notebook in Beethoven's lap. It read, *We're leaving now. A gentleman is here to see you. Shall I send him in?*

"Where is he from?" Beethoven asked.

He could not say. He speaks very little English. I believe he is from Japan.

"Japan? Why not? Send him in."

Stephen left the room and a few moments later, a small man, barely taller than the chair Beethoven sat in, entered. He wore a black top hat that added about a third of his height to the top of his head. He dressed like a proper Englishman.

The man removed his hat and placed it on the piano top. He then bent deep at the waist and bowed before the composer. Beethoven offered a quick nod and handed him the notebook.

"What's your name?"

The man squinted.

"Your name," Beethoven motioned to himself, "I am the composer Ludwig van Beethoven. You?" He motioned to the small stranger.

The man's eyebrows raised, and he took the pen and pad from Beethoven. He wrote, *I am Heppiri Otoko.*

"I suppose it would be hypocritical of me to suggest your name is difficult to pronounce. Why are you here, Mr. Otoko?"

I am Heppiri Otoko. I help you listen.

Beethoven snorted. "Ah, you are responding to my call for physicians. Mr. Otoko, I hate to disappoint you, but you are too late. I lost my sense of hearing two months ago."

Mr. Otoko took up the notebook again as deep thought spread across his face. *I show you how to listen, not with ears.*

Beethoven snatched the notebook from Mr. Otoko's hands. "Mr. Otoko, I'm going to assume you did not come here to insult a deaf man and that your suggestion is a simple error in translation."

Mr. Otoko raised his hands in apology. Beethoven raised his

own to nudge the small man out of his bedroom. In one fluid motion, Mr. Otoko slid his fingers around Beethoven's wrist, turned his body to face away from the composer, and brought the composer's hand down to rest on the seat of his pants.

"What the devil are you doing?" Beethoven shouted.

Before he could struggle his way out of Mr. Otoko's grip, the unmistakable sensation of reverberations struck against the back of his hand. Mr. Otoko was passing wind.

Beethoven struggled at first, but when Mr. Otoko let loose his grip, he left his hand in the warmth of the gas pushing against his skin. There was something familiar about the sequence with which it pillowed into him.

It was not a simple burst of wind. There was rhythm in it, tempo. A look of realisation crossed Beethoven's face, and he stumbled away from Mr. Otoko, retreating to the window and wrapping himself in the thick curtains so that only the top of his head was visible.

"That was my sonata. That was my Piano Sonata Number 17 in D minor. Wasn't it? I felt it. I did not hear it, but I felt it," he muttered into the heavy drapes.

Mr. Otoko remained silent.

Beethoven slid the fabric back from his face. "How?"

Mr. Otoko picked up the notebook from the floor and wrote, *I am Heppiri Otoko.*

"I know that! How did you...play my sonata?"

Heppiri Otoko use vibrations so you listen.

"Vibrations? You play music with your intestinal wind." Beethoven stepped out from the curtain. "Mr. Otoko, is this your profession?"

He nodded.

"Fascinating. Utterly fascinating. But as much as I...appreciate you showing me this, it is not how I compose music. I do not wish to learn what you do, Mr. Otoko."

I show you vibrations. Piano same as wind.

Beethoven raised an eyebrow. "I'll indulge you, Mr. Otoko. Show me."

Mr. Otoko reached into his jacket pocket and produced a thin wooden rod and then sketched something in Beethoven's notebook.

The sketch was of a thin line between two globes. Mr. Otoko pointed with his pinky finger at the line and, with his other hand, displayed the wooden rod. He then pointed to the globes and, with the rod, motioned towards the seat of his pants. Beneath the sketch, it read, *This how Heppiri Otoko teach vibrations.*

Mr. Otoko flipped the page. He drew another sketch of the wooden rod, but this time placed it between two lips.

Place between lips. You listen piano vibrations.

"Mr. Otoko, it occurs to me you may be a clever prank sent by a friend to cheer me up. I suspect Stephan will jump into the room any moment now."

Mr. Otoko stood still and silent.

Beethoven stood still and silent.

"Give me the stick then," Beethoven said at last. "To be clear, this rod hasn't been...used?"

Mr. Otoko shook his head with a smile.

Beethoven opened his mouth and slid the wooden rod between his lips and clamped down with his teeth. Mr. Otoko directed him to the piano. Beethoven wiped sweat from his brow with the back of his hand and took a seat. Mr. Otoko pressed a key on the piano and, with a sideways glance, waited for Beethoven to react.

The bewildered composer shook his head.

Mr. Otoko went a few keys further across the piano and pressed several of them. Beethoven again heard nothing.

Mr. Otoko positioned himself behind Beethoven and pressed a finger to the back of his head with some force. Beethoven could do nothing but comply and found himself bent over, a mere inch from the keys. Mr. Otoko reached around Beethoven's head and applied pressure on the ends of the wooden rod, which brought his mouth in contact with the keys he had never known this intimately before.

Then Mr. Otoko returned to his former position and, with some bit of drama, wound his finger through the air with a minor flourish before bringing it down to play a B sharp.

The hammer struck the string, and the vibrations rattled through the keys and into the rod. Beethoven's teeth buzzed before the sensation travelled through his skull and down his spine like firecrackers on a wire. He leaped from the piano, wide-eyed and looking like a mad devil. His mouth dropped open, and the rod fell from his lips. He laughed. It was deep and booming as if saved up for this moment. And as quickly as it had come, it left him. His eyes turned red and tears ran down his cheeks. He walked to the piano and placed his hands on its top. He sat down and sobbed.

Mr. Otoko placed his hand on Beethoven's shoulder.

"I can feel them! My god, I can hear them. They are the tail end of the echoes of my voice shouted back to me down a deep dark well, but I hear them."

Mr. Otoko produced another wooden rod from his suit jacket and placed it in Beethoven's hands. They spent the entire evening in this manner. Mr. Otoko playing single notes, Beethoven feeling their light course through his waking mind, still too scared to produce the notes himself.

Gerhard, stunned by these revelations, scribbled in the notebook, *And what of Mr. Otoko?*

"I searched for him. I sent inquiries to my musical contacts in Japan, but they produced nothing. He took the notebooks he had written in and the wooden rods he had used. I was forced to use a wooden spoon once he left. I did, however, discover that his name was never Heppiri Otoko. That was the name of his profession. Flatulists, we would call them."

It's almost as if he was never here at all.

"Indeed. He truly came and went...with the wind." Beethoven's face twitched as it had earlier, but the tired muscles stretched into a smile this time.

"Ludwig, are you filling my son's head with that gassy stranger story?" Stephan bellowed from the doorway.

Gerhard looked to his father, putting the truth together. He shot a disappointed look at Beethoven, who had turned to face Stephan. The old composer chuckled to himself.

Gerhard grabbed the notebook and wrote, *Thanks for the story!*

Beethoven continued to laugh, amused with himself. Gerhard and Stephan waved their goodbyes and left the composer to his work.

He stood from his piano and walked his tired body to his clothes cabinet. He opened the thin wooden door and reached into a box on the lower shelf. He pulled out a black top hat, which was almost a third of his entire height, placed it atop his head, and returned to his piano.

WHERE THINGS ARE CONTINUALLY DAMAGED

A Lamplighter lit streetlights, illuminating the shadows that darkened cities as the sun went down. As electrical systems replaced gas lamps, lamplighters disappeared and, with them, the need for their profession.

THE SUN HUNG low in a cloudy cradle as the pair shut the door on their new home. His son adjusted his cap and kicked a rock down the empty street. It rattled against a rusted pipe alerting a few ravens to their presence.

"We have always been in love with light, George," he said to his son as he locked the door.

"Who?" his son asked.

"All of us. Every one of us. We even speak of it like one we love. We say we lose light as if it is something precious, like love or time."

His son walked a few paces ahead before turning around to face him. "We can lose darkness too, da," George said.

"Nay, we don't lose darkness. Darkness spreads, like disease. We chase it away like a rat. We were born to dark places, but we fell for the light and ever since we have been lighting our homes and our streets to rid our lives of shadow. Light is security and we are its providers," he said, slipping his thumbs beneath the straps of his overalls.

"Who?" George asked again.

"Us. The lamplighters, son. We're important and this is why I'm showing you all o' this. So you can do it too." They walked further down the street, passing several darkening doorways until they reached a narrow alley.

"What if I don't wanna?"

"Why wouldn't you want to?"

"I ain't tall enough."

"You will be. Today, I'll lift you up."

"What if I don't wanna be lifted up?"

He placed his hand on his son's shoulder. "Enough, George. Here, take this key and fetch my pole from the shed."

The boy took the metal key and, for a moment, considered it as a nesting mother robin might a twig, before setting off into the alley, fading into darkness. He appeared a few minutes later, stepping sideways between the walls with the pole held above his head. "What now?" George asked.

"We'll light the lamps on Saint George Street and then go north up Cannon Street and do the same.

"Only two streets?"

"That'll be more than enough for your first time. We'll circle around so you can go back home and help your aunt with your cousins."

The pair left their home on Chapman Street and walked south towards their destination. A foul odour floated through the deep blue-hued streets of London. It was strong tonight, and it stuck to their skin and clothes and he sighed, knowing the smell would follow them home.

"I don't like 'em," George grunted.

"Who?"

"My cousins. She treats 'em better."

"Give them time, George. It's difficult bringing two families under one roof. It was a special kindness to let us live here."

"And she ain't my ma."

"I know. She isn't trying to be."

They walked in silence until they arrived at Saint George Street. A few dockworkers stumbled across their path, startling both parties.

"Our apolo-apologeese, mis-ter," one of them said.

"Get home to your wives, you daft lot. It's getting late," he muttered back. The men laughed and continued on into the purpling light.

The sound of hooves striking stones echoed around them, drawing his attention back to the street. Several pairs of horses pulling black carriages raced by them, driven to get home before the sun set. He waited until traffic settled down and then at last all that remained was him, his son, and the perpetual stench of the River Thames.

"These lamps are newer. They run on gas, so it's a simple place to start. I'll show you how to do one and then you can try," he said, as he motioned for George to follow him to the first lamp.

He brought the end of the pole down in front of George's face. The brassy end still shone in the violet light. "See that wick? We'll light it and then use it to light the gas in the lamp." He pulled a match from his pocket with his free hand and struck it along the shaft of the pole. The shadows pulled back and a small flame rushed in to fill the void. He held it to the wick until it caught, then shook the match until it lost its light.

Grabbing the pole with two hands, he manoeuvred the glowing end into the opening at the bottom of the glass casing of the lamp. With a few quick turns, it took some of the fire and a star lit. It blushed and grew until its light filled the casing and spilled onto the street like yellow rain forming golden pools around their feet.

"I ain't never seen one when it lights. It's beautiful." George was unmoving, captivated by the shimmering ball.

He looked down the street. It was almost black now. "Step into the light, George. Stay close to it now." He flicked his fingers to get his son's attention, and the boy made a small jump forward.

"Would you like to light the next one?"

He handed the pole to George, and the boy wrapped his small hands around it like it was holy, as if he had never seen one before this moment.

"It's important to keep your wits, George. The darker it gets, the more dangerous this task becomes." He looked to the next post and knelt down so his eyes met George's. "Do you hear that?"

"I understand, da," George said.

"No, I know you do. Do you hear *that*?" he said.

They were both quiet. George held his breath. The street was empty. The river, choked with sludge, bubbled as it strained to push through London's clogged arteries.

"I don't—"

"Shh!"

Then it came. A clicking sound, wet, and hollow, a thin membrane being popped in quick succession. Then it went quiet again.

George's eyes went wide.

"Shh...don't scream," he said.

"Have you ever seen one?" George whispered.

"No. They don't come out much now. Your grandfather saw them, though. He wouldn't say what they looked like."

"Did they ever hurt him?"

"No, I don't think so. Something must have hurt *them*, though. Your great-grandfather told me they used to leave the river, take form, walk the streets. Now, they huddle away from us in a dark so thick we haven't seen one for years."

George grabbed his hand.

"What are they?"

He tugged on his son's arm to get him to move.

"I don't know. People used to say it was a plague from the river, but they were here before the water grew toxic. Your grandfather thought they were spirits trapped in London."

"He did? That's not what spirits look like."

"No? What do they look like?"

George paused before saying, "Not like that."

Several sticky pops rattled off the facades of the surrounding buildings.

"Da?"

"Mhm?"

"I'm glad something hurt them."

"Let's get to the next post. We're already behind."

They continued lighting the lamps along Saint George Street. The sound had rattled the boy, so he didn't light the next few lamps; he had his eyes trained on the swelling dark around them. At the foot of the fifth post, he took the pole and, having climbed on his father's shoulders, lit the lamp himself. They felt the warmth bathe them both and the golden light coated their skin until it was without blemish, mark, or wrinkle.

They continued on, George lighting each of the remaining lamps on the street. Once the last one was lit, he celebrated by swinging the pole through the air like a sword. The darkness swirled against it, rushing to avoid the luminescent tip. The motion doused the wick.

He frowned at his son. "I forgot my matchbook."

His son's expression changed.

"Don't worry, there's more in a small box attached to the next lamp. We'll light it again there. We're going right at this crossing, up Cannon Street. Be careful, now. We'll have a break in coverage. It'll be dark for a brief time."

"I'm scared."

"There's nothing to be afraid of, George. I do this every night. They're as scared of us as we are of them."

"Why do they hate the light, da?"

He reached for his son's outstretched hand and brought him in-step. He walked from the yellow light into the darkness. Their footfalls were the only noise. It was twelve steps from this spot to the next. He had counted many times. He looked down at his son but his eyes hadn't yet adjusted and he saw nothing but a small black mass moving alongside him.

At six steps he thought he saw something shimmer darkly, pressed up against a nearby wall. At the eighth step, he felt a small tug on his arm and realised George had stumbled trying to keep up with his adult stride. He pulled the boy along, never loosening his grip. At the tenth step, the familiar click and pop of wet muck, multiple clicks, from multiple places. He ran the last two steps and swung George forward. The boy landed inches from the post.

His eyes pulled in as much moonlight as they could and in the grey of Cannon Street he could have sworn he saw black water shifting around their ankles, curling around their shoulders, licking the dry hair on their heads.

He fumbled taking a match from the storage box. It was damp and took a few strikes before it lit. His son's face glowed and the shadows, real and imagined, shrank back around them, scattered to the gaps and spaces and places in between.

"Who says they hate the light? Maybe they love it, more than even we do."

"But they run from it, da. They must fear it." George returned to a whisper.

"I don't know. Sometimes when you love something it's hard to be near it."

"That doesn't make sense."

He chuckled and lit the first lamppost. The pair, breathing easier, continued along Cannon Street, away from the river and its fetor.

"This street is older. No gas here, just candles. They can be a bit of a fuss, but I've always liked their glow a little more."

"Kids at school say London don't need lamplighters anymore."

"What do you think?"

George's eyes roamed the surrounding twilight. "I think we still do."

"Only a few of us left. There's more of them now. The darkness has grown while we've become few."

George looked up at him.

"It doesn't matter, though. One day these lamps'll light themselves and they won't need any of us and the river will swallow the dark for good."

They walked to the next lamppost, and George climbed back onto his shoulders and pushed the pole inside its casing. It took a few moments longer to get the wick to light, but soon the candle flickered to life and filled the globe with an amber gleam.

They lit the entirety of Cannon Street. The red brick buildings on either side of them appeared warmer with the added light. A few faces appeared at windows. A small child looked out at George and his father and waved to them.

"That's all for now. You can run home. Stick to the path. Stay in the light."

"Will I have to do this without you?"

"Someday."

"Hopefully not until I'm taller."

Either way, you know what to do now. Here, take the pole and lock it up when you get home."

"What will you use?"

"There's a shed nearby. I'll grab another one. This one's yours now."

George hugged him and gripped the pole in his hands. He gave his father a slight nod, the kind a man gives another man, and walked back down the street he helped light. The boy's dark outline shrank until the light swallowed it.

He was alone now. The street was quiet again and there were no faces peering out from windows. He leaned against the lamppost and reached into his coat pocket. He felt the frayed edge of paper meet his fingertips and he pulled it out, the photo stained yellow by light and time. He ran the back of his small finger against the cheek of the woman he cradled in his hand.

He lost himself for a time then, only pulled from these thoughts by the sounds of shadows slogging through the streets in the distance. He replaced the photo and regained his composure with a hearty sniff.

The shed was nearby, lit from the inside. Still, he struck a match and approached, careful to shield the small light from the wind and growing fog. He rifled through his pockets for the keys, and after several bad picks, produced the correct one. The match had burned down to his fingers, and he felt the sting of its heat. He swore as he dropped it and stuck his finger and thumb into his mouth and let the placebo of saliva nurse the burn.

He swore again before lighting another match and unlocking the door. It trembled as it came unstuck and swung open. The small light cast itself into the shed. Roiling shadows, clinging to the floor, walls, and ceiling, peeled away. He wasted no time finding the rod and reached for it.

As he pulled it down, the wind whipped in from behind him. A sound like mucus breaking in a fit of coughing soon followed. Darkness creeped over his shoulders and cool air pricked the hairs on his exposed arms. He spun and met with an impenetrable shadow. The sight caused him to stumble back, falling against a worktable, before scrambling to regain his balance and raise the match.

A liquid fixture fell into the suggestion of a man. Its edges blurred, undefined. It had no face, no features. It did not move, but he could hear it breathing. Phlegm-riddled and sick, its head turned to face him and it stared without eyes. Its arm reached out, still unmoving. Shadows in the room pooled together, helping the appendage grow.

He shook with panic. A thin tendril arced through the space

between them like ink through water, but stopped short of his hand. It hovered above the light, a long, wispy finger. It held its position, its movement stilled and silenced. The finger swirled around the flame as if tracing its dancing edges, stroking it. Eventually, smoke rose from the finger. It swelled, then popped like a blister.

There was a noise then. Not a sign of pain, something else. Then it left him. The shadows retreated through windows, the door, whatever open spaces they found.

He snatched the rod and scampered back into the streets, returning to the golden light of the lamps. His eyes burned at their brilliance, already accustomed to the dark. He buckled over, trying to catch his breath, trying to understand what he had just seen.

Darkness and a heavy fog filled London's streets now. The dread would not leave him even after he pushed the encounter from his mind. There were still so many lamps to light. He finished an hour later and returned home.

His sister and her children crowded around a roaring fire. She was reading to them when he arrived and smiled when he entered. George was sleeping nearby. He took a seat away from the fire, in the shadows near the window. He rubbed his burned fingers together, felt the hot blister growing beneath his skin and marvelled at the brightened streets like it was the first time he knew their warmth.

He had always loved the light. He always would. He always would.

HOWEVER, REPLIED THE UNIVERSE

The Leech Collector procured medicinal leeches for the use of bloodletting in 19th-century Europe. Collectors often used their own arms and legs to attract leeches from nearby bogs, causing many to die of blood loss and infection.

THE LEECH WRITHED like a diseased tongue between Ronald's wet fingers. A slice of silver moonlight flashed across its body.

"Do you ever feel bad for 'em?" Ronald asked, adding the leech to the coiling mass already in the jar that hung from the front pocket of his overalls.

"For who?" Dale asked.

"The leeches. We've emptied the whole of Britain. We're gonna have to trade with the French soon. The only place with any left is this marsh."

"No, Ron. I don't feel bad for the leeches. I feel bad for us being out in a marsh at midnight pulling these bloodsuckers by the light of this shit lantern that won't stay lit. That's who I feel bad for."

Ronald took another jar and slid it into his front pocket beside the other.

"Hey, Dale, who am I?"

Dale raised the lantern to cast some light on his colleague. Ronald had his hands pressed against the bottoms of the jars, pushing them up like breasts.

"An arsehole?"

"No, ya twat. Tits!" he shouted, pointing at the jars.

"Hilarious. Top drawer stuff, that."

Ronald shrugged and began waving his lantern across the surface of the swamp.

"So you don't think we should let these buggers make more babies before we snatch 'em? It just seems cruel to me."

Dale straightened and kneaded his lower back. "I'm doing what I'm told, Ron. I don't know if it's wrong or if it's right. I know I have a job and that I can afford a home and to feed my family and that's all I need to know."

"It's a good job, alright. Fresh air, I get to use me hands, and I feel like I'm saving people, y'know. I mean, these little guys are going to go suck the sickness right outta some poor infected sap. He'll be right as rain in the morn' and a little o' that is because of us, Dale."

"I suppose," Dale replied, bending over again to run his hands through the dark water for his quarry.

"If a giant came to your home though, tore the roof off all savage-like, and grabbed your wife and your sons and threw 'em in a jar, I believe you would be right angry, Dale."

"I guess it's a good thing there's no such thing as giants then."

"I bet the leeches tell their kids there's no such thing as giants, too." Ronald plunged his fist into the water. "Then their roofs get ripped off and they're all thrown in a jar!" He pulled it back out with force enough to splash the both of them.

Dale waited for the water to calm again, his annoyance going unseen in the dark. "We're human beings. It's not the same."

"I just hope we don't have some karmic debt to repay after all o' this."

"Karmic debt?"

"That funny Indian bloke who's always hangin' outside the pub with those flyers for Buddha or whatever. He told me about karma. It's like getting what's owed to you. If you're an arse like you, watch out, Dale. Karma's gonna get you."

"That's not karma, that's natural consequence. If I spit in your face, you punch me. That's not karma, that's consequence, Ron."

"Just saying, Dale. That Indian made some good points. Don't get me wrong, I'm a Catholic through and through, but Jesus never said nothing like karma."

"Yes, he did. It's one of the most famous scriptures. The golden rule. Do unto others and all that."

"Hmm, yeah, I suppose I'd never thought of it like that."

"How did you think of it?" Dale asked, raising his lantern to see his partner.

"I guess I didn't. You hear something every Sunday fer your whole life it just becomes noise after a while. Then you hear an exotic thing like karma and it's like sleeping with a new woman all over again." Ronald laughed as he thrust his hips into the air.

"Can we get on with this?" Dale asked, motioning to the swamp.

"Sure, sure. They're bitin' now," Ronald said, wincing into the night sky.

"Let them have their fill this time. The batch from last night was a wash. They died before they were transported."

Dale raised his left leg from the black water and brought his lantern down towards it. The amber light cast a warm glow onto a pale leg covered in throbbing black globs of gelatinous leeches. The surrounding skin was angry and red. Blood dripped down Dale's leg from under each of the worms as they fed in abundance.

"Get 'em for me."

Ronald sloshed through the water as he pulled a set of steel tongs from his belt. He bent over and held a jar under the leeches. One by one, he squeezed each leech with the tongs and pulled them from Dale's leg. Most of them wouldn't release their bite without force. They left small gashes in the flesh. Dale's leg was a mess of swamp and blood by the time the jar filled.

"How do you feel?" Ronald asked.

"I'm fine. Let's get the other one done before I pass out." Dale rolled the leg of his coveralls down over his bleeding leg and cinched it at the ankle.

They repeated the process on his other leg.

Dale leaned on Ronald for support.

"You alright?" Ronald asked.

"Just a little light-headed. Gave 'em too much that time. Let's get yours done."

The pair performed the same process again on Ronald. His legs, more muscular than Dale's, could hold more leeches. He bled more too, but felt fine afterward.

"We should use the horse legs for the rest of the night, Dale. You don't look too well and I don't want you passing out in this swamp. They'd drain you before you drown."

Dale nodded, and they trudged back to their wagon. In the back, amongst spare jars and oily rags, were two horse legs tied in cloth. Blood had seeped through the wrappings.

"The butcher ever ask you about these?" Dale said, some colour returning to his cheeks now.

"I told him I use them to feed my dogs."

"You don't have dogs."

"I think it sounds better than telling him I use them to catch leeches."

Ronald unwrapped the horse limbs and handed one to Dale. "One for you; one for me."

As if neither of them wanted to reach their destination, they dragged their heels back to the swamp. They dipped the bleeding end of their horse legs into the water and stirred the muck like a soup for several minutes, drawing the leeches from the water to the bloody stump.

It was quiet, the only sounds were the occasional slop of water or the suck of air being pushed out of thick sludge taking its space. Dale's lamp swung back and forth from his wrist. A breeze passed over the swamp and snuffed it out. Dale cursed.

In the dark, Dale's black silhouette twisted against the blue backdrop of night. A slice of silver moonlight flashed across his body.

Then a small stone, red with heat, fell from the sky and struck Dale on the top of his head, ripped through his body, and burst from his pelvis. The rock struck the surface of the swamp, it floated, on fire, then sank.

Dale grunted, smoke wafting from the hole in his head, singed flesh and innards steaming inside the cauterised wound in his gut.

"Dale!" Ronald screamed. He dropped his horse leg into the water and the swamp swallowed it.

Dale's head twitched and then his body fell forward into the swamp. It hit the thick water with a splat and the murky water swallowed him, along with his own horse leg.

Ronald looked up as the sky was torn open and fire streaked across idle stars. Dozens of tiny sparks flashed into existence and fizzled out soon after they appeared, passing over without incident.

Ronald held his position in the mire alone, transfixed by the beauty, by the horror.

THIS GLORIOUS THOUGHT

Sin eaters consumed ritual meals left on the bodies of the recently deceased. The meals were thought to have absorbed the sins of the dead and would therefore be transferred to the Sin eater, absolving the soul from guilt. Sin eaters were despised as it was assumed they grew more vile with each ceremony.

Victor Leung
1624-1665
Beef, bread, water (requested)

He was my first. The grave marker's engraving was smoothed and worn by heat and cold, and some encouragement by my hand, to make room for my additions. Moss grew at its base, as it did on them all.

Victor drank far too much the night he died. He stumbled from the tavern and into farmer Fleishman's fields. He lifted a scythe from an unlocked shed and cut down every last head of cattle. The farmer caught up with him, though. Bashed his skull in with the flat side of a hammer. It was the end for Victor, and the beginning for me.

I had no one by then. My wife, Sarah, died months earlier. The plague took her first. The second was my son. I thought I would be third, but God saw fit to spare me for something much darker.

Victor's death was sudden. He had no chance to confess and absolve himself of his ultimate sins. Ours was a good Christian village and we couldn't abide the idea of a man dying outside the grace of God. His family posted a notice for the village's first sin eater. I answered the call, but I couldn't, or wouldn't, have told you why.

Victor's family knew me. They knew what happened to me. They treated me like a dear friend when I arrived at their home, showed me to their dinner table where they laid Victor's stiff body. There was so much more hair than I expected. A sheet lay across his lower half for modesty. The corpse was white at the edges and grew bluer the closer my eyes drew to the middle. It reminded me of the ice core I pulled from the lake when ice fishing a few winters earlier. I did that for a meal too.

His family placed a small handkerchief across Victor's chest and placed on it three pieces of bread, two of which were end pieces, and what looked like a dry slab of beef.

I could have just let it be. I didn't have to tell them that to do it correctly, the food must touch the skin of the deceased to absorb the sins into itself. I didn't have to tell them. Did I care if Victor went to heaven? No. I did tell them, though. Victor's wife sobbed, but she pushed one of her sons forward to remove the cloth. It's difficult to balance three pieces of bread and a piece of meat on a bloated rib cage. It took his son, Klaus, several tries before he could step away from his father's body.

I felt nothing for Victor. I did not know him. It's strange to say that in a village of only a dozen families. My movements were affected with an air of general ritual, none of it necessary. It's what

I would have wanted, the appearance of something holy and redeeming.

I approached the body with reverence, my head down, hands clasped in front of me as if silent prayer propelled each step.

The bread was nestled in a mass of hair, but I still ate it quicker than expected. It might have been the first proper food to reach my stomach since my family passed. Despite that, the meal was still plain, the bread dry, the beef tasteless. It's difficult to cut a tough piece of meat on the chest of a dead man. So I picked the slab up and bit into it with my back teeth, tearing smaller pieces of leathery animal flesh into my mouth.

"Water," I whispered over my shoulder. Victor's wife fetched a tin pitcher and poured water into a cup for me. I half-smiled in appreciation. I don't think I would have been able to swallow the meal without it.

This, of course, was well before I began spreading the lie that the greater the meal, the greater the chance at redemption.

I completed the meal and turned to face Victor's family. Grief clung to their faces like dried mud, but it did not hide the disgust in their eyes.

From that point on, I became the village sin eater, but also outcast, a pariah, only summoned when needed. Which was frequent, as the plague spread deeper and farther and claimed the lives of others.

Roslyn Guthrie
1650 - 1666
Salted herring, fava beans, water (requested)

After Victor, I turned to drinking. I saw his icy body in my sleep; I ate his flesh until there was nothing left on the dinner table and in the worst of these nightmares, I would eat his family, too. So I drank to dull my senses and sleep a dreamless sleep.

Roslyn passed almost a full year after Victor. Her family did not move her from her bed. She died in her sleep before a priest could be called in to hear her confession. She reminded me of my wife. Same red hair matted to her wet forehead. I tried to look away. She was young and exposed when I entered the home. I asked that they place a sheet over her breasts, but her family seemed desperate to ensure we did the ritual right. Take no chances, they said.

I kneeled beside the girl. Leaking red sores like the blistering mouths of volcanoes erupted from her stomach and down the fronts and backs of her thin, white legs. Black veins ran under her skin like tunnels mined through flesh and blood.

Despite this, I did not fear her. If I succumbed to the plague, I would join my wife and son.

Roslyn's family left herring and beans on her chest. The fish, two thin strips of pink and silver folded over onto themselves inside a ring of green fava beans, was a most appetizing platter. I would need water after the salted fish, so I asked for it. I ate the meal with delight, which I realized after was wrong of me. Families do not want the sin eater to enjoy ingesting the sins of their loved ones. So I paused in deep reflection for two full minutes after licking my fingers clean. As I counted to one hundred and twenty in my head, I stared down at Roslyn and thought she looked pleased. I wondered what she could have needed forgiveness for.

Helen Leung
1601 - 1666
Chicken, carrots, water (requested, but denied)

Helen was Victor's mother. She died of natural causes, a rarity. She left the faith late in life, but her daughter-in-law convinced herself she could save her mother-in-law's soul post-mortem.

I confess I don't believe in what I do. It was a way to punish myself, I think. Then I saw the comfort it brought families, and it became a duty. They all despised me, but I needed no friends. I was already alone, so I could at least be useful.

For a second time in this home, I kneeled beside the bed. It was more difficult this time, as my belly had grown despite being active and eating very little. My knees cracked as I got into position and studied the body. Helen's skin was thin like the feather-plucked flesh of a chicken. When I picked up the chicken leg that lay on her chest, a few of the carrots fell from her body. Her breasts, sagging to the left and right so far her nipples were beyond view, jiggled in a way that reminded me of a jellyfish. The image made me sick, and I gagged over Helen's body, but swallowed the small amount of bile that rose in my throat.

It didn't impress the family, and they rushed me through the eating, not as concerned with ritual for Helen the heathen. I asked for water, but they denied me and sent me on my way. Klaus, a year older and a year stronger, spit on my clothes as I left.

I felt strange that evening. I walked the road back to my home and the muscles in my chest ached like they were bruised. A deep and sudden fatigue settled into my bones then, and I remember needing to piss more than I ever have before.

There were thirty-seven people in the village. The following year there would be only one.

Günther Hardwick
1630 - 1667
Game pheasant, beef, chicken, pork, corn, wine

It took me a year to bury the last body in the village. If there were any as deserving as I to be a sin eater, it would be Günther, a common thief with no formal address. He would come through the village for a drink, rob a home or two and be on his way. No one saw him commit any crimes, but it was always the case that when he strolled into town, families would notice a few things gone missing.

I wasn't sure of his guilt until I caught him here at the graves looting the dead. He was three feet deep into Klaus's pit when I smashed the broad side of my shovel over his head. I didn't intend on it, but it killed him. One more sin to pile on the ghoulish heap already contained within me. I dragged Günther from the hole and dug him a new one. It was only fair to eat his sins too, since I didn't give him much time to confess, after all.

With everyone in the village dead, I took whatever food was in their storage and prepared a feast on the body of poor Günther Hardwick. I cooked a large pheasant, a pig, chicken, cow, every animal I ever knew. And I drank too much wine. In fact, I never stopped drinking wine since Victor, but I drank even more that night. I ate and drank until I could not consume another morsel and then I rolled over and fell asleep.

When I woke, my head hurt and the branches above me spun round until I grew queasy. I closed my eyes and dug a grave for Günther. I buried him and covered his pitiful body with dirt and slumped back against a large oak tree and fell asleep once again.

Sarah Wolfram
1635-1664
Bread, wine

Jonathan Wolfram
-
Bread, wine

The sun woke me. My clothes were wet from the morning mists. I had thrown up on myself during the night, so I took my shirt off, climbed the oak tree, and crawled my way out onto one of its sturdiest arms. The whole village spread out below me. Nothing moved any longer. Not a single soul remained save me. Not a single chimney puffed with smoke. It was as still as an oil painting.

My eyes drifted downward to the grave markers. I buried all of them. Three generations lay below me. Forty-two souls without a blemish, pure as untouched snow. All of their sins and secrets hung from an oak tree above them.

It wasn't forty-two souls, though. As I scanned the plots, I realized I only serviced forty of the bodies, for we buried my wife and son before I became a sin eater. That partly pleased me, but mostly troubled me. So I scrambled down the tree and found the shovel that Günther used the night before. I stood in front of Sarah's grave and uprooted grass and root until my tool struck wood.

With the edge of the shovel's head, I pried the first few nails out and a small gap formed between the lid and the bottom. Something should have stopped me, but I wouldn't allow it. The shovel continued down the length of the lid, wrenching nails from their decades-old home.

What I saw didn't match what I expected. I don't think it did, anyway. She was dust and bone now. We all look so alike in death. It's our skin and our eyes and our hair that allows us to tell one from another, but underneath we all look like Sarah. And Sarah looked like every one of us.

I slid my hands under her, cradled her skull in my left arm and supported her legs at the knees with my other. I laid her at the foot of the oak tree and noticed two of her ribs popped out of place where her stomach had grown. The space where Jonathan would have been when she passed was so small, and it made me glad he passed with her. It was harder to know her and lose her than to never know her at all.

If there is a meal more holy than bread and wine, I do not know it. I've stated my disbelief already, but if there's a chance my actions could still save them, this was best. The damp bread I placed on Sarah's ribs, but for the first time I did nothing symbolic, nothing sacred. I thought of my wife and my son and how unnecessary this was for them. Swallowing the bread was almost impossible as my chest and throat spasmed as I tried to hold back tears. Her skinless face leered up at me and made me uncomfortable with what I was doing, but I got it down.

I laid them back in the coffin and pushed the dirt back into the hole, sealing it forever. Now my task was done.

James Wolfram
1632-1667
Scraps, wine

Who eats the sin of the sin eater? Even if anyone else survived in our village, I would have asked none of them to take that burden. There's no telling what it would do to someone who believed they were actually inheriting evil.

I took off my clothes and lay in the spot where Sarah had moments before. I grabbed a few loose scraps of leftover meat and vegetables and piled it as high as I could on my chest and then tipped a bottle of wine over my face and let it pour through my beard and run down my neck and cool my back as it soaked into the earth.

Salvation without help is the most pathetic act of all, I realized. I prayed. Thousands of silent words, some not even my own, swirled through my polluted mind and, after a time, mingled with audible ones that escaped my lips without notice. Gruff, guttural moans and gasps started out loud and then became quiet as a whimper. A pack of wolves howled from deep within the forest, around the village, or perhaps closer.

THE SUN ALSO SETS

A Lector was a hired reader, often found in cigar factories, tasked with reading books and newspapers to entertain the workers.

"WHAT'S that got to do with it? I had no experience writing a novel until I wrote the first one. Tell them it's yours and they'll know you're an author. Then write the next one and you'll already be an author."

I rolled the stem of the daiquiri glass between my thumb and finger and stared into the shifting opaque liquid. It was good advice. I quit stalling and tipped the glass back and swallowed the lot. No, that was too much. It came back up in a coughing fit.

"I'm going to do it. I'm going to stop telling them it's yours and I'm going to tell them, tell all of them, the book is mine," I said.

Hemingway slapped my back, "Good for you. Get us another round."

The torcedores were already at their rolling stations before I entered the factory that morning. My novel, its loose pages moist with sweat from my hands, rolled like one of their cigars. I tried to act cool, said hello to all the usual people. I nodded at Ernesto, Luis, waved across the floor at Javier. They must know already. It felt like all twenty of them knew I had been lying this whole time.

I wound my way through the rolling stations, each one already piled high with scraps of tobacco leaves that always looked every bit like chocolate shavings. I never grew tired of the aromas, the reddish-brown hues, the sound of artisans in deep focus rolling the large leaves.

There was a time I worked in a bread factory, a manure plant, and a coffee plant, and while at least one of those isn't intended to smell pleasant, they all became obnoxious over time. Tobacco, though, was different to me every morning. The dampness of the sun-grown leaves the torcedores used as wrappers were thick with the smells of earth and Cuban mud, some with sugar. The capote and seco, the filler leaves, folded and placed with precision to burn at different speeds, were potent with rich aromas that made my head light every time I walked by. I rarely smoked cigars, but I was still addicted. The volado, the ignition leaf, chocolate brown like the rest but infused with a bitterness that was unmistakable to me now, reset my olfactories each time.

The scents had me lost in thought when I knocked a small jar of vegetable gum from a nearby rolling station. It was from the factory's sole torcedora. I apologised to her, and she smiled back. I had not learned her name yet.

All of them rolled with such skill and grace, the act never grew stale to my eyes. I realised for the first time as I reached my chair that if revealing the truth caused them to reject me, I would miss this place.

I lifted a foot to the first rung of the small ladder I used to reach the top of the lector's chair.

Luis shouted from his station, "More Hemingway today, José?"

I turned back, summoning the conviction instilled in me the night before by several drinks and my contemporary, "Not quite."

"Is it true?" Hemingway said, slapping my manuscript on the bar.

"Well, no, it's fiction," I said.

"Of course it's fiction. I don't believe for one second you could be FAR. You don't have the body or the eyes of a military man."

I opened my mouth to speak, but he went on.

"I meant, is it true and honest? Does it respect and honour the ones involved? That is the only good thing a writer can do," he said, the last few words drowned in his daiquiri.

"Yes, it is true and honest. The characters are based on friends and the stories they told me. I believe I honoured them."

Hemingway came around to sit on the same side. He put his heavy arm around me. It was awkward to speak now. He leaned in close and his white beard tickled my ear.

"Then you have done a good thing," he said in a rum and lime soaked whisper, before slamming a fist on the table. Our glasses nearly tipped and a few pieces of cutlery fell to the floor.

I allowed myself a small smile before remembering why I had sought the author out.

"The thing is, Ernest, Mr. Hemingway–"

"Everybody calls me Papa!"

"If it's all the same to you, I'll stick with–"

"Papa! Good choice," he said, bringing a new daiquiri to his nose, letting the whiskers of his moustache dip into the drink first, like a cat exploring someplace new.

"Okay, Papa, the thing is, I'm a lector. I read to the workers at a cigar factory while they roll. It helps pass the day for them. They all chip in and I make a good living doing it. I've been reading them several of your stories and, well, one day I read one of my own."

"Excellent. A writer must have his words read or he is no writer at all."

"I agree, however, I was afraid they wouldn't want to hear my writing, so I told them it was one of your stories."

"You're a fool, José! How good a book is should be judged by the man who writes it. If you believe it to be good and true, they will hear it as good and true."

"I should have had more confidence. Knowing that you think it's a fine story—"

"I never said it was a fine story. I asked if it was true."

"Oh, well, is it good?"

"José, my wife and son are away and I am alone in Havana and I am several scotches and daiquiris into a very fine evening. I could not tell you if your story was good if you paid me. Which you haven't, so I am even less inclined to."

Hemingway rose from his seat, but turned before leaving, "The first line is very good. It will be a fine story if the rest holds up.

Wiggling into the high chair, I made myself comfortable, adjusting the pillow I sat on and laying my manuscript across my lap, opened to where we had left off. I stared down at the page before starting. I continued for nearly two hours, pausing only once for water. My throat, emboldened by the coming revelation, seemed to lubricate itself with the adrenaline coursing through me. It was difficult to know if my audience was enjoying the story. At one point, during a particularly touching section, the torcedora raised her head and looked up at me. I started to sweat.

During the lunch break, I sat with them, my head still buzzing with my unshared secret. I watched them as they ate. Luis chewed with his mouth open, but said nothing. The torcedora was shy. She also said nothing. Ernesto and Javier argued about the football match, but soon grew quiet as they filled their bellies. Perhaps...no, could they be in quiet reflection after hearing my story? No, that would be too perfect. Surely not.

We returned to our spots after the break. I was shaking in my chair, unable to keep the secret in longer. I began reading again. It took another three hours to complete. When I reached the last line, I placed my feet on the highest rung of the ladder and stood up, squeezing the bundle in my nervous hands.

I took a breath and read the ending. I folded the page over and gripped the stack of paper in my hands with the care of a torcedore and a finished cigar. "Written by," I paused to observe my world, capture it less it became unrecognisable, "José Borges!"

The words flew from my mouth with a shout. I held my hands outstretched beside me, palms facing the tin roof. My name bounced off the metal walls with electricity and charged between the worktables like a bull. I could have sworn the stacks of leaves trembled at my proclamation. I let the pages fall to the floor with a thud and awaited my audience's reaction.

Not a single movement.

"Written by...José Borges!" I shouted again.

None of them looked up from their task. Not even the torcedora, who had been so enraptured by my words earlier, noted the reveal.

The floor manager, Carlos, opened the door of his small office and shouted, "José! Quit shouting! I'm on the phone. You aren't a right, you're a privilege. If you're a problem, you're out."

He slammed the door behind him.

Luis looked up from his rolling, "Hey José, what's with the shouting? Keep it down or we'll lose you."

"Didn't you–," I lowered my voice, "Didn't you hear what I said? Written by José Borges."

"Yeah, we heard you. What's the big deal?" Javier asked.

"What's the big–guys, it's me! I'm José Borges! I wrote the story you've been listening to all day."

They looked stunned. Javier looked over at Luis in confusion. It was dawning on them.

"Your last name is Borges?" Javier asked.

"Yes, of course it is. I've been here for months. How did you not know that?"

They both shrugged their shoulders.

Ernesto piped up, "Same as that writer from Argentina. What's his name, José Luis Borges?"

"What? No, that's Jorge Luis Borges. That's not the same at all. He's Jorge! I'm José!"

"Who's José Borges?" The torcedora asked.

"Me! I'm José Borges!"

"I thought your name was Ernesto," she said.

"That's me. I'm Ernesto," Ernesto shouted across the room.

The torcedora shrugged and went back to her rolling.

"Oh, what do you know! No one even knows your name," I shouted down at her.

"Come now, José. Don't be unkind. She's new here," Javier said.

"I just want to make sure everyone knows my name is José Borges. I'm not Jorge Luis Borges."

"That Borges, he's a wonderful writer. You should bring some of his stories in next week," Ernesto said.

My shoulders dropped.

"My name is—"

Carlos's door opened, and he poked his head out. "José! You're fired. Too much shouting."

"You need a fine last line too," Hemingway added. "And you need several more in between. Do you have that?"

"I think— I know I do."

"Then you'll be great." He turned back towards the bar with a few parting words over his shoulder. "In the end, it doesn't matter, anyway. They'll forget all of us, José. They'll forget you. They'll forget me too. Does it matter when?"

POWER IN THE NAME

A Nomenclator was a slave tasked with remembering the names of the people his master met during political campaigns or social events. They would whisper details into the ear of their master to make them appear more knowledgeable and personable.

A nomenclator has no name of its own.
A nomenclator need know nothing but the names of all others.
A nomenclator's entire being is in service to The Master.
Names have power.

THOSE WORDS WERE BURNED into the wooden ceiling of the nomenclator's small chambers. He woke to them, slept to them, lived them in all hours between.

The boy stared at the wall opposite him and adjusted his position on the thin mattress. He mouthed a word, sending it across the room on a gentle breath, letting it land amongst the feuillemort rug beside his bed.

He had not known his name until this morning, when a letter, slipped between the iron bars of the window set high on the far wall, fell into his chamber. He opened it with care, having never received one before. The paper was damp and smelled of mothballs. The letter contained only four words: Your name is Jonah.

He mouthed the two syllables again. The *O* stretched his cheeks inward, and the *ah* relaxed his jaw. *How fun it is to say your own name,* he thought. *How soothing it would be for others to experience it.* He dared not say it aloud.

His smile faded as he remembered the scorched words above him and his heart became heavy in his chest. His duty was to know the name of all others but himself. The Master relied on him, needed him. He slid the letter and envelope under his flimsy pillow and left his chambers. A feast was about to begin, and his skill would be required.

He climbed the stairs to the banquet hall and slid through the doorway before taking his position beside it. Pink-veined white marble was the material of choice for the entire hall. Purple velvet cushions lay against the arms of several creamy white sofas scattered about the perimeter. Jonah leaned into a vase of red and white roses near him and inhaled the powdery scent.

Guests filed in one at a time. He made a mental note of each one as they did. No surprises. He knew them all. Jonah was unknown to these people, but he was a legend amongst the nomenclator class. He was born into this life and trained at a young age. He could, in an instant, recall the names and matching faces of over four hundred of the elite class. This was a massive social advantage for the Master, who never found himself caught without a name on the tip of his tongue. *Names have power.*

He traced the letters of his own name against the brown sackcloth pants he wore. He wanted nothing more than to scream it, bathe others in his pleasure.

"The Lord and Lady Dhich!" the man-at-door bellowed. Two plump, glazed faces went flush at their introduction and the aristocrats took a few seconds to gain their composure before waddling across the room to join the other guests. As the room filled, it appeared more like a psychedelic renaissance painting. These elites moved little, but they chattered in hushed tones laced with intrigue punctuated by the occasional ostentatious wave of their arms. Their clothes were regal and colourful, their moustaches oiled and slicked, their faces powdered and lips rouged. In the same way, the women wore hair that defied gravity and dusted their cleavage with glitter to attract the eye.

"The Lord and Lady Laebea!" Another glistening, panting pair entered the room.

Jonah had seen the guest list earlier. There would be no others. The Master would arrive soon. Jonah was sweating. The knowledge of his own name teased his tongue, dared it to form the first consonant. The pit of his stomach was white hot and tight. He felt strange, transformed, as if he would burst, spraying his guts onto the faces of all around him. Drench them. Drown them in the warmth of all he was. He shook his head, steadied himself. *Jonah.* He swallowed and clamped his jaw shut. His tongue was stiff, resisting, but subsided.

The door beside him opened, and The Master stepped through. He wore a black robe embroidered with gold leaf that hung from his shoulders to the floor, covering his feet.

Jonah announced, "The Master of the House, Lord Cummington of Two Hills."

The Master strode into the room, ever unphased by the sound of his name. Those in attendance nodded and gave him warm applause.

Jonah went to work and took his position beside The Master, who was already making his way into the thickening crowd. He reached a hand out to Lord Sixtenigne and Jonah, like a phantom, whispered the man's name into The Master's ear.

"Lord Sixtenigne, it is a pleasure," The Master said.

The Lord almost buckled at the knees at the sweet sound of his own name as it left the reddened lips of The Master.

"Lady Sixtenigne, I regret my wife will not be joining us this evening. I may have need of you on the dance floor."

The Lady grabbed her husband's wrist. She shut her eyes and bit her lip, her breath left her flared nostrils in a sharp staccato.

Jonah's heart rate sped up. A dampness grew under his arms. He longed for his name.

The Master moved through the frothing crowd and greeted another pair who Jonah provided names for. They, too, left with their eyes rolling back in their heads.

Jonah. He wanted to hear it. He needed to hear it. He bit his tongue and tried to ignore the impulse.

The Master reached out for the next group and Jonah, flustered by his thoughts, stumbled on the names. "Lord and Lady Jo-Dawgee."

"Lord and Lady Jo-Dawgee. It is always a pleasure," The Master said, before Jonah corrected his mistake.

All pomp left the hall. The Lord and Lady Dawgee recoiled and turned to one another, horrific expressions marred their painted faces.

Jonah leaned in and said, "Lord and Lady Dawgee. Just Dawgee. They performed a duet during the feast of Summer Solstice."

The Master twisted his old head to the side and stared into Jonah's eyes. There was a crease between his eyebrows that was so deep Jonah wondered if light ever touched the skin there. The Master was not pleased. Jonah would be punished.

"My apologies, Lord and Lady Dawgee. In my excitement to mention the delicious duet you performed last summer, I seem to have stumbled over your names. Forgive me."

Their names and the compliment washed over the Dawgees' faces like a shadow being expelled by light. The din in the room grew again and the Master, recovered, moved on.

Jonah could not steady his mind, though. His mouth moved

without his meaning to. He wished he had never learned his name at all.

The Master leaned into another handshake and Jonah was late to arrive. A moment of confusion preceded his whisper, "Lord and Lady...uh...Bellowjhub."

The Master, annoyed, smacked Jonah away before sending another set of guests into pure rapture.

Jonah resolved himself to finish the night strong. The Master reached the next pair and Jonah was at his ear within moments.

"Lord and Lady...Jonah." The name left his mouth, and he stumbled backward, eyes wide. Death would be the punishment for this.

The Master's crimson lips bunched together like blooming snapdragons, followed by the relaxing of his jaw. He didn't even hear his name, but his body registered it. The letters entered him and his stomach clenched and his legs spasmed before the sensation rode up his spine like champagne bubbles. He grunted and fell to one knee. The colours of the room swirled and mixed like a painter's palette and then he was prostrate on the floor. The marble cooled his cheek. Hands were on his shoulders, they rolled his body over. He did not feel them; only euphoria coursed through his veins, feeding his muscles, exploding like tiny fireworks behind his eyes.

"He's positively catatonic," Lady Laebea said.

Jonah saw The Master's leathery face appear above his own. The Master pressed his ear against Jonah's mouth and his grey hair fell onto his face.

"Hmph. Get me another nomenclator. Throw this one into the sea," The Master said.

Another boy, clad in sackcloth, approached The Master. The new nomenclator stepped over Jonah's still body and the soft scent of mothballs trailed behind him as he moved on and out of his peripheral vision.

Jonah could not move and didn't want to anyway. His eyes

filled with light and his mind and body pulsed with a delight he had never known. It consumed him so completely that when they took his body to the parapets of Two Hills castle, he did not even resist being thrown over the edge. Nor did he feel the whoosh of air that came to meet him as he plummeted to the rocks and raging waters below. Nor did he fight for air when the waves overtook him and pulled him below the surface. Nor did he struggle when the ridged beak of a giant pelican scooped him from the sea and he slid into the magnificent bird's throat pouch.

An hour later, his body unclenched and the light faded from his eyes. It was dark and moist in the pelican's pouch. His head rested against something wet and sticky. He pulled away and bits of shredded membrane clung to his cheek. He tried to stand, but the bird's constant swaying made it impossible to gain a footing.

"Hello!" he shouted.

"Hello *croak,* " the pelican said.

"I'm in your pouch. I'm a small child," Jonah said.

"That's preposterous - *squawk* - I do not eat children - *croak* - I eat fish."

"The people of Two Hills threw me into the water and you scooped me up in your beak."

"If they threw you into the water, then you must be a fish and not a child - *cough* - for only fish are thrown into water - *squawk* - you seek to trick me into opening my mouth and then you will leap from it and swim away."

"No, I won't. Well, I do seek to leave your mouth, but only because I'm not a fish."

"I knew it - *squawk* - If you are not a fish then why were you in the water?"

"The Master of Two Hills, Lord Cummington, had me thrown in after I failed to name his guests."

"Why did you fail?"

"I learned my name and could not resist hearing it. When the Master said it, I froze with glee. It was beautiful to my ears."

"Yes,well - *cough* - this is a strange story for a fish to tell but I am also starving. I will make you a deal - *squawk* - I will not swallow you for three days and three nights. If you can guess my name within that time I will open my beak and let you leave - *squawk* - If not cough I will swallow you."

"You are gracious, noble bird. I will guess your name."

On the first day, the pelican tossed Jonah around the inside of its throat pouch. The walls of its gullet were soft, and despite the frantic pace of the day, Jonah put several hours of thought into an answer to the question that would set him free. He was unsuccessful, though.

It was difficult to maintain his thoughts as the pelican swooped through the air and dove into the water for more sustenance. A gush of water, a pair of herrings, or a clump of seaweed regularly joined Jonah.

"Hello," Jonah would say to the herrings.

They splashed and struggled. Fear filled their eyes.

"Hang on trickster fish, *squawk,*" the pelican warned before draining the water in its throat pouch and swallowing the herrings.

On the second day, the sounds of other pelicans made their way to Jonah. "Are you nesting?" he asked the giant bird.

"Yes - *cough* - I have not seen my family in some time. I missed them."

Jonah smiled and pressed his ear up to the mucous membranes of the throat pouch and strained to hear the bird introduce itself to others or to hear other birds address it. Unfortunately, the pouch had poor acoustics and allowed little sound to make its way into the belly of the throat.

"Do you miss your family trickster fish?" the pelican asked later that day.

"I never knew them. The Master is my family. I need to prove myself in his court."

"Why would you want to return to one who is not your family -

croak."

"I must take my revenge on the boy who stole my spot by his side. He tricked me by telling me my name."

"Hm - *cough* - how did he know your name?"

Jonah paused for a moment.

"So the name you thought was yours may not be yours at all, *squawk?*"

Jonah didn't sleep well.

On the morning of the third day, Jonah woke to frantic squawking. The throat pouch thrashed left and right and the boy flipped onto his head several times.

"Great bird? Are you okay?" he asked.

"I have caught my sensitive beak in a fishing line - *squawk* - trickster fish!"

"I can release you. If you'd only let me out, I can release your beak."

"More deception, trickster fish - *squawk* - You think me a fool?"

"I do not. If you are trapped, then so am I. If you release me, then I will repay you in kind and you will see that I am not a fish and we will go our separate ways."

"I will think on this new deal - *cough* - trickster fish."

"And I will let you think."

Jonah felt good about the new arrangement. The pelican could not escape without his help and would see reason. He sat down in the sticky muck around him and the sliver of blue sky he could see from where he sat turned into a sliver of silver.

"Trickster fish - *croak* - have you guessed my name?"

"Ronald? Simon? Wesley? Herbert?"

"None of these."

"Then no, I haven't. Have you considered releasing me to help you?" Jonah replied.

"I did - *squawk* - Your proposal is tempting, and I meant to release you but I fell asleep in the afternoon sun. Now my belly grumbles as I have not eaten in some time - *squawk* - I must address my most pressing need so I decline your proposal and based on our previous arrangement I will eat you now and hope for rescue later."

Before Jonah could protest, the pelican thrashed against the fishing line and shook its beak until Jonah's grip faltered and he fell into the pelican's stomach and was devoured.

The pelican chuckled. It had no name. It was a pelican.

EXPOSURE

Employing the first publicly available means of photography, Daguerreotypists used a complex five-step process to produce images on chemically treated plates of metal or glass.

Polishing—

To ensure the highest image quality, the silver side of the plate must be polished to a mirror finish. There can be no blemish or other contamination present when the plate is sensitized, so polishing should be completed immediately before use. If lampblack or rottenstone is available, use these first. If not, animal hide or velvet will suffice. Finally, use nitric acid to burn away any remaining organic matter.

EDMONDE RUBBED moisturizer onto Azélie's cheeks and forehead; he ran his long, thin finger down the bridge of her nose.

"Rub it in, gently, circular motions," he said, miming the action.

Azélie did as instructed, careful not to move anything but her arms. It took Edmonde almost an hour to achieve the pose. Her body, pale as powdered sugar, draped across the velvet chaise like a polar bear skin rug. One leg stretched out flat across the cushions, toes pointed. The right, raised at the knee, leaned over the other like a sloping hill. Her back arched. The gap between her skin and the curved mahogany armrest was important to Edmonde. She rested her upper back on the arm of the chaise, pushing her breasts out and upward, nipples surrounded by the soft pink petals of a begonia, pointing to the ceiling. Her head hung over the edge, her long black hair teased the wooden floor. With her left arm, she spread the moisturizer onto her skin.

Light leaked into the room and pushed the darkness up towards the ceiling, where a heavy chandelier hung like a crystalline spider. Golden-framed portraits of lords and ladies hung on every inch of the walls. Azélie recognized none of them.

Edmonde slid a small wooden stool next to the chaise near her head and held a silver pocket mirror over her face. She had missed a small glob of the animal fat on her forehead. She smoothed it across her face with two fingers. Her cheeks were flush and her lips heavy and plumped with lipstick smeared across her cheek as if someone had smacked her with the back of an angry hand.

Edmonde scooted the stool even closer until he appeared, upside-down, above her, looking into her eyes and blocking her view of the chandelier.

"Keep your eyes open," he said, producing a small dropper filled with a clear liquid. "It's belladonna. It will keep your pupils dilated."

Azélie forced her eyelids open wide and watched as each drop fell into her eye. Edmonde's face grew cloudy before she blinked it into focus again.

He raised his hand, two fingers covered in a black paste. "Now close your eyes. I'm going to put this on your eyelids. Don't open them until I tell you. It's soot and water, so it'll sting if it gets in your eye."

She coughed. "Am I a whore this time?" she asked.

Edmonde closed her eyelids with the palm of his hand. "You're perfect this time. As you are every time."

Sensitization—

In darkness, expose the polished silver surface to halogen fumes to increase the sensitivity of the silver halide coating. Bromine or chlorine work best, re-fume with iodine fumes if desired.

Edmonde pulled on the gold-threaded cord and the heavy drapes separated. Searing light entered the room and struck the chaise. Azélie moaned. Her eyes burned, her drugged pupils unable to shrink away from the light. She shielded her face with her hand.

"Edmonde, close the curtains!" she shouted.

"It's part of the scene, my love."

"I don't like the light. You know that. I don't like you seeing me in the light."

She heard Edmonde's footsteps, his figure like silvery smoke through her blurred vision. His fingertips glided up her thigh and the tiny, invisible hairs on her leg went rigid.

He pressed a finger into her skin and traced crooked lines up and down her legs. On any other woman, it would have been a random path, led only by his intuition and the trembling in his excited hands. On her, deep blue veins mapped the route for him, pulsing just under the surface, warm and filled to bursting with disease. He continued to follow the lines up her waist. He dipped down her side before coming back around to her abdomen. His wrist brushed the small patch of hair between her legs and she closed her eyes.

The light made her skin translucent, thin, honest, her sickness revealed to the camera that stood only a few feet away.

She gasped.

Exposure—

Once inserted into a plate holder, slide the sensitized plate into the camera body and remove the dark slide to expose its surface. When your subject is ready, remove the cap from the camera lens to begin the exposure. Depending on chemicals used, the light present, and the power of the lens, the required exposure time will range from a few seconds to several minutes. Experiment with different options to find the time that produces the desired effect. When satisfied, replace the lens cap and the dark slide to once again keep it from the light.

Azélie's body shuddered and her legs shook, threatening to alter the precise position. Her lower back and feet cramped. Her chest grew red and hot under her icy fingers. Edmonde moved to the foot of the chaise and soon his warm breath made phantom contact against her inner thighs. Azélie lost herself in the thousand shards of glass above her, the crystal reflecting her sex to dozens of portraits of dead men and women hanging on the surrounding walls.

Edmonde retreated to the camera, ensuring the moment when her body, near death, shook with the terror of life and captured her forever in silver dust as delicate as that of a butterfly's wing.

Development—

The silver plate must be exposed to the fumes of heated mercury to produce an observable image. This will require several minutes inside a developing box. Alternatively, the effects of several days of development can be achieved by exposing an iodine-only sensitized plate to sunlight passed through yellow or red glass. The silver iodide will not be affected by the light as it is insensitive to the red spectrum, but the blues and violets taken in by the camera during exposure will be revealed through the sunbath and the image will appear.

Edmonde closed the drapes, and Azélie relaxed her position. Her body was damp with sweat. She sat up and covered herself with a silk robe.

"How do you feel?" Edmonde asked.

"I feel whole," she said.

"You aren't as close to the end as you thought?" Edmonde asked, taking the camera apart and placing the pieces into a velvet-lined case.

"I'm much further away than I thought," Azélie said with a smile that went unnoticed.

"We'll have more time for these sessions then. I have a few other concepts I'd like to try with you, but we'll have to wait until you're closer to the end. The sickness adds a desperation to your face that I want to capture as it worsens."

"Edmonde, I'm no longer sick. The doctors say it is a miracle. It's going away, slowly, but it is going away," Azélie said, her face searching Edmonde's profile for a glimmer of happiness.

Edmonde did not speak. The side of his face that she could see was in thought. His brow furrowed, his lips forming a bit of a frown. He walked over to her and kneeled in front of her. He clasped her hands, and finally, his lips curled into a thin smile.

Fixing—

Once the image has been developed, use a mild solution of sodium thiosulfate to remove the remaining silver halide to ensure the plate is no longer sensitive to light. If sodium thiosulfate is not available, a solution of common salt may also be used to less effect. Finally, treat the plate with gold toning to warm the image. It will bring life to the subject and will reinforce the silver particles. Pour the gold chloride solution over the surface of the plate, heat over an open flame, drain, rinse, and leave to dry.

Something was different. It was in his eyes. His smile was genuine, but she knew his yearning for her had dissipated.

Azélie stood, her silk gown open just enough to show the delicate lines of her breasts; the scent of her hung thick in front of him. Light from a far away room cast a soft glow on the curves of her hips and the muscles in her stomach. She pulled him to his feet and slid her hand down the front of his pants. He was soft. All thrill had left his body.

"I'm sorry," he whispered. "Now that, well...this all just feels pedestrian." He finished packing up his equipment. "I believe our time together has concluded." He picked up his camera case and left.

Azélie stood alone in the great room. A hundred reflections in the chandelier above captured her finger tracing the blackness of her veins. All but one. In that reflection, her veins grew ever darker. The sickness consumed her flesh and her body drained of life, dried up, and Edmonde was still with her, pushing her forward, to the moment he might find her beautiful.

AFTERWORD

Authors were individuals who wrote books, plays, screenplays, and other forms of publications to be read for entertainment or informational purposes.

A BITTERSWEET, nutty aroma stretches out across the room and settles into worn fabrics and dark corners, wrestling the stench of week-old Chinese food from Garrett's nose. His high had faded.

Madeline shifted under the sheets beside him, her exposed leg pressed against the tablet lost in the folds. A screen powered on, enveloping the bedroom in contrasting warm yellow light and offensive sound.

Garrett felt his way under her body for the remote. She moaned at the intrusion. He turned the volume down just as the monitor filled with a woman's face. She was flawless, as if she had skipped several generations of evolution and was now without pores. Her chestnut hair was pulled to one side, draped over her bare shoulder. Her white dress was elegant and tight around her body. She stood in endless light, a faint shadow around her figure, the only visible clue she was not a floating head. A Welsh accent entered the room with the ease of an old friend.

"English held out the longest," she started. "Despite its popularity, or perhaps due to it, its complexities and inefficiencies helped it endure. However, it wasn't enough to outpace us. It was, in time, used up like all the others."

Madeline twisted herself around to see the screen. She grunted and flopped her head back into the pillow.

An obelisk, onyx and featureless, replaced the image of the woman. It floated above a crowd of gathered people. They reached towards it like baby birds to their mother. The sun glinted off the tip of the column and a panel slid open on its side. A blinding light poured from the door and bathed the crowd.

The woman's voice returned. "This fall, we welcome the next stage in human development. We welcome renewal of the imagination. We welcome the future of language."

A countdown began. Words appeared in the background, out of focus, teasing what was to come.

"UPC is gonna put you outta work, Mads," Garrett said, squeezing a sticky black block of opium between his thumb and forefinger.

Madeline rolled over again, and this time sat up. She took a drag from a pipe on her bedside table and released it towards the screen. It swirled outward like an apparition reaching towards the ticking numbers. It broke apart as it met the glass.

"Then I guess you'll have no reason to come here anymore," Madeline replied.

"You aren't my highest paying customer, but you are always the most pleasant," Garrett said.

"Shit, Garrett. Just let me enjoy this. I'm paying you. Here." She grabbed a small flash drive from her bedside table and tossed it into his lap.

"The last one you gave me was pretty light. You find anything good this time?"

"It's old English, forgotten, but it's English. That's more than you'll get from anyone else. Now if you don't mind, fuck off. I'm trying to forget all of...," she motioned around the room, "this. That includes you."

Garrett pocketed the drive and the remaining opium. He leaned over Madeline with the familiarity of a lover moving in for a goodnight kiss, but instead reached for his pipe.

"I am right, though. I shouldn't expect many more of these drives if they actually launch the new language when they say they're going to."

Madeline sighed and rolled over, stuffing her face into the dark folds of her pillow. "They won't," she said.

"Replaying log 43.2257 - Miles Tiller."

"Since activating the A.I., I have been uploading all writing in the public domain to its systems. Preliminary results show rapid cataloguing of data, as expected. Unexpected is how quickly the system has already made its prediction. It's difficult to say how accurate it is at this point with only a fraction of the world's literature within it, but even so, the estimate is a lot sooner than I would have guessed.

"Madeline suggested I name the A.I.. It was a dig, but I think I might. Dicto, after the family dog, Ditto. Seemed clever. I'm sure only a software engineer would think so."

"End of log 43.2257 - Miles Tiller."

"Rumours swirl, Albert. They are saying the Universal Publishing Coalition, that great and holy union of elitist pricks like yourself, have made almost no progress in almost a decade," Iosefa said, a smile smeared across his face so wide you could almost hear how much he was relishing this moment.

Albert laughed, swirling ice cubes in his glass with the tip of his finger. "I've always loved that one. It started a year after we began and it seems to get refreshed around the UPC's anniversary. I must admit, I expected more of you than to buy into gossip."

Iosefa leaned forward in his chair. "I buy gossip when it reeks of truth, Albert."

"Did you ask me here just to regurgitate the rags for me?" Albert asked.

Iosefa laughed. He was a large man, Samoan, and his laugh bubbled in his throat like the hidden molten innards of a dormant volcano. "I asked you here to throw you a life preserver."

Albert furrowed his brow and opened his arms.

"You may not admit to me now that the UPC has failed, but take a message back to your friends. Tell them that Iosefa Latu, founder of the Company of Lexis, has not only completed the evolution of language, but has written a manuscript born of it."

"Bullshit. That cult of yours is nothing more than a bunch of desperate fans and linguist hacks who didn't make the UPC's grade. Your approach is asinine, your methods ugly," Albert barked.

Iosefa leaned back in his seat, his eyes locked on Albert's face, as few did. "Tell me, what happened to your nose?"

Albert balked.

"You say my methods are ugly to you, but between the two of us, I am the only one with results. In fact, the only ugly thing here is that hideous wound on your face. So tell me, because I've never heard the story."

Albert, self-conscious, wiped his leaking nose with a cloth napkin. He snorted. "Frostbite, you ignorant shit. That's the entire story, and I can only assume it's still better than the drivel you wrote using whatever gibberish you designed in that compound of yours."

"Frostbite. I've never felt a real winter. It's a foreign concept to me. Your skin grew over the wound, though? There are no rough edges or dry skin, just a gaping hole I can see inside. It makes me nauseous just to look at you, old man. I can smell the rot emanating from that crater where your nose should be."

Albert wiped his face again.

"Tell me again that the UPC has succeeded in its mission to mass-evolve the earth's languages."

"I owe you nothing, Iosefa. The UPC will reveal its work in two weeks. Your work will be forgotten. You will be forgotten. The world will move on under my language, not yours." Albert held his napkin against his face, sniffling.

Iosefa tossed his own napkin across the table. "Did you know that when a man lies, his blood pressure increases? It causes our nose to grow, like Pinocchio. It's much too slight to notice in real life, of course. However, the catecholamines that are released irritate the mucus in our sinuses and our nose runs. Unfortunately, because of your deformity, you have no way of stopping the flow."

Iosefa stood. He towered over the old man.

"In other words, I can see that you're lying, Albert."

"Replaying log 54.2257 - Miles Tiller."

"I have given Dicto access to the world network and he...it, has already begun scraping sites identified as carrying large amounts of literature. Most of the early sites were housing terabytes of fanfiction and self-published material. It has since circumvented the security in digital storefronts and has downloaded the entirety of published works up to the 23rd century. Security appears to be stronger for current works.

"What is troubling to me now is that I have asked Dicto to adjust its deadline algorithm in real-time and even without having analysed modern literature, it has predicted we have already run out of time.

"We have already written every possible combination of words. It estimates that 3% of all English literature is unintentional plagiarism. If these numbers are correct, everything published since 2255 has more or less been a copy of some other, earlier, work. Incredible."

"End of log 54.2257 - Miles Tiller."

Madeline felt electric, a combination of whatever was left in her system and a lack of sleep and a proper meal. Her patrons flickered into the room, their appearance a mixture of human, animal, and fictional avatars. They took seats around her kitchen table. In reality, it could only seat four, it now sat ten. Their images overlapped at the elbows. Her head hung low and swayed back and forth as if she could hear music, but there was none.

Madeline placed her hand on the glass surface of the table and the tip of her index finger pulsed with a faint blue glow as it authenticated her identity and collected her stored data. Her remaining patrons entered the room and took a seat.

"Ladies, gentlemen, it has come to my attention that my production has not met your expectations," Madeline said, still looking downward, the table lighting up now with the contents of her personal storage.

One of them, an upright cartoonish unicorn with a rainbow mane, said, "We pay you well for your work, Madeline. We knew results would be difficult to come by, but not this difficult, especially considering your father. Your name carried a lot of weight. It was a major motivating factor in my investment."

"I told you at the start that I would not be using my father's A.I. to help with my research. I'm a professional dictoresearcher and, while slower, I'm able to access areas that a program cannot."

Another patron, with the tiny-moustached face of a centuries-old war villain, spoke, "And yet we see fresh allotments landing on the free market all the time. We aren't questioning your skill, bitch; we're questioning your integrity."

The other patrons muttered amongst themselves and Madeline, sensing a turn, started a private chat with the visage of Adolf Hitler.

"This is how this conversation is going to go. You're going to claim I'm withholding or selling usable language from the patrons. I'm going to deny it. Then after some arguing back and forth, I'll grant you first rights to view and 30 days to release new material in the," Madeline scanned a list at her fingertips, "North American market before I release to the other patrons. In exchange, you continue your support and, when we exit this conversation, you attest that we spoke about professional decorum and respect for one another. Do you agree, you utter piece of shit?" Madeline asked.

Hitler grunted. "I accept."

Madeline swiped a hand across the table and brought the rest of the patrons back into the room.

"My apologies to the rest of you. I know I am at the mercy of your patronage, but I do not tolerate disrespect."

"I'm also sorry. It was a dick thing to say," Hitler said.

"Thank you. I assure you the next time we meet it will be to bring you usable words, not excuses. Good night."

The room went dark again as she closed the communication. Her account balance, illuminated in red beside her, turned to green as her patrons left their payments before logging off.

Madeline tapped a finger on each of the seven USB drives on the table in front of her. Their plastic casing felt almost foreign, ancient. It was the only way she could keep the words she'd found off the network, away from the A.I. She sighed. She told herself this was the last time.

"Replaying log 63.2257 - Miles Tiller."

"Dicto has been creating abnormalities. I noticed the first one when I realised the amount of data I had uploaded to it didn't match what it was reporting. At first I shrugged it off as an inefficiency in compression. It was only a few kilobytes. Since then, it's grown. Again, it's not much, but it's clear there is a small amount of data being sectioned off by the A.I. and it's completely locked it off.

"I can't be sure of the exact cause, but after a thorough diagnostic, I discovered a few lines of code introduced to its neural mesh during its build. I sent it over to the lab to have it analysed. It might let me understand what's going on with the locked away data.

"This would all be troubling enough, however, what keeps gnawing at me now is that the only person other than myself with that kind of access to Dicto during its creation would have been Madeline."

"End of log 63.2257 - Miles Tiller."

Iosefa ran a thick finger across the charred engraving on his desk's top.

"Are those the last words?" Garrett asked.

Yes, yes, I will be sure to handle the plums with exquisite care, it read.

"A daily reminder of my legacy. A gift from my publisher."

"It's better than the other guy. Albert Butts, was it?"

Iosefa nodded before breaking into a laugh. Both men said in unison, "Flipperdeedee, flipperdeedoo, it's all there is to do."

They continued to laugh, sweet smoke pulled into their lungs with each breath. Iosefa buckled over, an enormous bear in a man suit.

"What does that even mean?" Garret asked.

"Who gives a shit? He's genre. It never means anything."

"Don't you write science fiction?"

"Literary science fiction," Iosefa said.

Garrett laughed, but Iosefa remained quiet. Garrett choked on his cackles and stared at the large man as a white rabbit would stare at a wolf, hoping it had not made enough noise to rule out blending in with its surroundings.

After several heartbeats, which felt like 300, Iosefa chuckled before breaking into a deep laugh again. Even the walls relaxed.

"What's the number for?" Garrett asked, pointing beneath the quote.

"0.0002%. It's the percent of original words in my novel. Even though his line was migao, Albert's novel was 0.0003% original because his word count was lower."

Iosefa took another drag off the joint he was sharing. "That's how he slaughtered me in sales. His publisher went on a media blitz and drove the readers wild for the most original novel left on earth. Mine reviewed better, but it didn't matter. Reviews don't sell books.

Iosefa placed his finger on the woodgrain and his finger lit with a soft purple light. The tabletop faded and the text of his new novel appeared in front of him under the glass surface. He ran his finger down the table and scrolled back through some 90,000 words.

"And this one?" Garret puffed.

"100% original. No one has ever written a novel like it. Swahili, German, Russian, Latin, Greek, dozens more. All languages, pure harmony. A prefix from one transplanted to the suffix of another. Old words given new life; original words that capture emotions and concepts no man has ever breathed, all of it, in here. And this novel is just a sample of the new language. Others will take this, learn it, and surpass us all with works of art."

"It's going to be a lot to learn."

"It should be. We're talking syntax and grammar from nearly one thousand languages and it still makes them sing. This is the language we should have had from the very beginning. One language for all."

"When are you going to release it?"

"At the same moment the UPC releases theirs. When the world discovers the UPC has spent a century and developed nothing, there will be a vacuum of expectation. The Company of Lexis will release my universal language to fill the void and it will allay any hesitations the world has when they see there is already a novel written in the language."

"Teach me something."

Iosefa smiled, as if he had been waiting a lifetime to be asked that question.

"One of my favourites is not rooted in any language. One of my dictoresearchers found it in an archive of words and phrases created in the early 21st century. One of them, *nodus tollens,* the realisation that the plot of your life no longer makes sense to you, has haunted me ever since I learned it. My life no longer makes any sense to me. I go where it leads."

"As do we all, Iosefa." Garrett pulled a USB drive from his pocket and placed it on the table, over the purple words of the new world. "I suppose you won't be needing these for much longer, then."

"I'll take what you can get until the launch. Let's keep as many words out of the hands of freelancers as possible. They're a large market. We'll need as many as we can get in the early days. They're going to descend on this language like hawks. We'll help them learn it and keep table scraps of unused words like this from distracting them."

Garrett leaned back in his chair. "Flipperdeedee, flipperdeedo. That's all there is to do."

———

"Replaying log 64.2257 - Miles Tiller."

"It didn't take very much pressure. I think Madeline had been wanting to tell me for quite some time. She didn't understand the code she inserted into Dicto. She had one of her friends, some free market hack, write a few lines of chaos for her. We haven't yet broken into the area that Dicto is keeping from us, but from what Madeline told me, it seems to keep words to itself. As it discovers unused arrangements, it skims every 12th for itself.

"I'm unsure what it plans to do with the words. A troubling amount of its neural mesh is being dedicated to the growing area. I could wipe it, but part of me wants to know what an A.I. will do with the last of our language."

"End of log 64.2257 - Miles Tiller."

———

Garrett placed his hand against a featureless wall and a small section of it opened. A dull yellow light oozed into the hall from distant lamps.

"I've been here dozens of times and I can never see the door until you open it." Madeline said.

Garrett chuckled. "I live here and I can barely tell where it is. If you pay well enough to hide something, my guys will make it invisible."

The pair walked into the pale light. The air inside was thick and earthy. Madeline was sensitive to artificial ecosystems, and this one was especially machine-made.

"You know I grow this shit just for you, hey? No one else smokes it. It's such a pain to harvest, and the high isn't strong enough for most of my clients."

"Do most of your clients pay you with unknown arrangements of words they've stolen from their benefactors?"

"They do not. Which is the only reason I come in here every few days," Garrett produced an unusual tool from his pocket, "and slice these pods like I'm peeling the skin off a grape."

The knife had an unusual handle. The butt had been modified to fit four small blades. He used them to make tiny cuts in the bulbous green skin of the poppy pod. Milky white latex dripped from the incisions, but clung to the side of the plant.

"We'll save that for the morning." Garrett turned to another plant that had the same scored etches on its side. The latex had turned brown. He ran the edge of the knife up the side of the plant like he was giving it a close shave. He took the knife over to a dish and added it to a large clump.

"You want what I have right now?"

"That's why I came."

"I didn't have time to turn it all into morphine, so the block's a little smaller than usual. I'll make it up on the next one."

"As long as it gets me high tonight," Madeline said, eyeing the sticky block like a favourite meal.

"That it will, M. That it will." Garrett put the morphine base into a black bag that vacuum-sealed itself once he pressed it closed. "You want to get something to eat?"

"No, Garrett. Just once I want to come here, get my drugs, and leave. I don't want to fuck, I don't want to eat. I want to smoke this bag until I forget my name."

Garrett put his hands up in defence before handing her the bag.

Madeline tried to grab it from his hand, but he tightened his grip on it.

"You know it's not your fault, right?"

"You asshole. Don't act familiar with me just because I let you sleep with me a few times. Give me what you owe me."

She tugged on the bag and he released it. She left, her hands white-knuckling the opium, shaking with rage and hurt.

"Replaying log 66.2257 - Miles Tiller."

"It's writing a story. Dicto isn't taking words at random, it's piecing together the best unused phrases in order to write a story of original material. It's going to do what humanity cannot. It's giving me the scraps it can't use. I'm torn. I'm obligated to remain objective, but I can't help but feel like a proud father."

"End of log 66.2257 - Miles Tiller."

The bones in Iosefa's inner ear vibrated him awake. He hadn't turned his communicator off since finishing his novel. He knew offers would begin coming in from interested publishers eventually, but the call he received this night was unexpected.

It was Albert. He asked to meet, but there was an element of the unhinged in his voice. Iosefa could hear it in the conversation's pace. It was too quick. The desperation tugged on Iosefa's curiosity and he agreed.

"Come quickly. We must speak," Albert said, then disconnected from the call.

It was the middle of the night. Iosefa had drifted off in his study. A thin book, Italo Calvino's *If on a Winter's Night a Traveller*, lay splayed across his chest. It fell to the floor when he rose and startled him.

He lumbered towards his bathroom and splashed water on his face, fixed his untucked shirt, poured himself a glass of water, and stared out the kitchen window while drinking. It was dark outside, an overcast day had led to an overcast night and clouds now blocked the moon and the stars. He found his coat near the door, slid into it, and threw a scarf around his neck, thinking it might be chilly at this time of night. The front door made a perceptible buzz as it recognised him and opened, letting only darkness into the entryway.

A man stood outside his door, his back turned to Iosefa. The man spun around, his face covered. They both jerked back, startling one another. The stranger raised his arm and for a moment Iosefa thought he was reaching out to shake his hand. Then there was a tiny flash, followed by immense pressure in Iosefa's nasal cavity. Between that moment and the one in which he felt all of his weight touch the marble floor, he recalled reading there being a burst of brain activity after death and that, for a brief instant, your mind is aware that you are dying. This repeated in his consciousness like a boolean loop, his brain no longer able to move from this thought to the next.

"Replaying log 69.2257 - Miles Tiller."

"I refuse to terminate Dicto, so I negotiated with it to allow me access to its quarantined areas. I would give up my access to its systems and, in exchange, I'm able to read what it's writing. It's cumbersome to access. I've created a neural interface that allows my mind to link to Dicto. It feels a bit like being aware you're dreaming, but your mind doesn't pull you out at the moment of realisation. The eject button is mine to push. It's safe enough. Leaves me with a bit of a headache, but it's worth it.

The method it's constructing the story is astonishing. As it discovers unused phrases, it slots them into predefined locations. It does not write from beginning to end, it already knows the story it's trying to tell. Every word. It just waits until it's sure the phrases are unique in arrangement. There are large passages assembled already. I'm reading them out of context, but they are unlike anything I've read before. I expected to find it clinical, or technical, in nature. Quite the opposite. It reads more like poetry. It breaks words, creates them too, but in a way that is understandable. I can't tell if I'm watching a master at work, or a child, fumbling with tools it hasn't learned how to use.

"End of log 69.2257 - Miles Tiller."

Madeline hadn't visited her father since he was first brought to the hospital. She blamed herself, but part of her was also afraid he would wake up and see what she had done to herself. She saw her reflection in the window beside his hospital bed. The yellow lights in the ceiling created dark pits under her eyes, drawing out the tiny veins in her cheeks. She didn't remember the last time she'd taken a shower.

She couldn't look at him, had to look at him through the reflection. It was easier to pretend she was glimpsing a loved one out of the corner of her eye rather than seeing flesh and blood breathing through tubes in front of her.

"Okay, I'm here and I should have something to say to you, but I don't. I'm not sure what that means, but it hurts. These are my last words. I was hoping something would come to me, but I have nothing for you. I suppose that isn't anything new, though."

Madeline took several steps back and sat on the edge of the bed, keeping the entire scene in the reflection in the mirror. She reached down beside her leg and found her father's hand. She slid her fingers between his thumb and forefinger.

"I do love you. I know you loved me, too. We just never knew how to love each other the way each of us wanted to be loved," she said, and took in a sharp breath. "That's okay, now. You weren't great at being a father, but I wasn't much of a daughter, either. We could have turned out worse, I suppose."

Madeline stood and walked to the door. "You had a brilliant mind, dad. I won't take that from you. And I won't let you know a life in which you are anything but brilliant."

She left the room, walked down the hall, and signed a set of papers releasing her father from life support.

Garrett stepped into the entry and kneeled beside the large body.

"Where the fuck were you going at this time of night, 'sefa? Shit, you gave me a fright."

Even dead, the man was still imposing, his gravitas not yet dissipated along with his breath.

Garrett pushed on the body to be sure. Definitely dead. He breathed out. His night just got a lot easier. Pulling a knife from his belt, the limited light catching the four small blades in the handle, he pulled Iosefa's arm out from under the body. Placing it against the marble of the entryway, he lined the large blade up with the index finger and sliced through bone and tendon with ease. He pulled Iosefa's scarf from around his neck and wrapped the raw edge of the finger in it, the dying digit protruding from the folds like a small, sad bouquet.

Pushing open the office door, he noted how much emptier it felt without Iosefa in it. The man knew how to fill a room. He made his way to the desk and pressed the loose finger against the glass. The fingerprint activated and Garrett was inside Iosefa's sanctuary. He took out two flash drives from his pocket and placed them on the glass. In one, he transferred the new language files and Iosefa's new work. In the other, he put everything else. The rest wouldn't interest the UPC, but would fetch a price on the market to his more dedicated fans.

He scooped the drives into his pocket and retreated to the front door, stepping aside the body, where he dropped the finger back with its owner. It dropped with a sticky thud.

Madeline drove to her father's lab. The guard waved her in despite not being able to find her ID badge. He knew her, and she was a mess. There were a few fire blankets in a nearby closet, and she wrapped herself in one. She had been coming here every night for the last few weeks. Watching her father's face on these screens, letting his voice rattle around her head, trying to embed this digital signal into something physical that would remain inside her for a while.

She reached the last entry. How poetic, she thought.

"Replaying log 74.2257 - Miles Tiller."

I can't believe I'm saying this, but it's a wonder. It moved me to tears. I may be too close to this to not have some bias and I'm not the best judge of art, but this is a marvel. It's not quite complete, but it will be. A matter of days, I suspect.

I'm looking at the first original work produced in years.

I need to share it. Madeline would appreciate this more. Could probably tell me if I'm just a sob or if we've created something here. Hm. Incredible.

"End of log 74.2257 - Miles Tiller."

The video didn't end, though. There were still several minutes remaining on this one. Madeline smiled at her father. He was buzzing with the delight of discovery. This was when he was at his best. He was present, even kinder. It was pure joy to be around him during these periods. She watched as he bounced around his lab, making his way back to the neural interface he used to communicate with Dicto.

Turning from the monitor, she spotted the chair. She'd never used it. In some ways she was jealous of the A.I.. Madeline never made her father that happy, never impressed him in the same way.

What an absurd thought.

She threw the blanket off and approached the chair. Her fingers sunk into its soft leather arm rests. His prototypes always felt like finished products. She lay down in the chair and stared at the ceiling and took a deep breath before pulling the interface down in front of her. The electrodes on her temples would allow her to feel, not just see, into a virtual space where she could speak with Dicto like it was right in front of her.

Once she powered it on, her world went dark. It wasn't just lights going out. She turned her head to the left and right, black everywhere. Then a message displayed in front of her. She was in the system, but there was nothing else around her.

The message, displayed in a vintage green font, read "Initiate Backup?"

"Yes?" she said.

A progress bar replaced the message, and she watched it fill in a little more than a few seconds, then she returned to the darkness of the loading area.

After a brief pause, she saw objects filling in around her. There was a couch first, then a tv, a fireplace, a window, then an entire world beyond it. She recognised it. She was home—her childhood home.

Her virtual hands ran over the wool blanket draped over the back of the couch and felt the sensation of its rough warmth move from its digital edges into her mind. There was always a delay, a fraction of a second, imperceptible to most, but it was always the tell that none of this was real. *It's close enough, though,* her father would say. She heard a dog bark and Ditto ran into the room panting, a ball clenched between glistening teeth. She pet his soft curls and threw the ball into the adjoining room, and he left to chase it. Madeline opened the screen door and sat on the porch steps, marvelling at the accuracy her father put into the skyline of the city.

"He sat right here, too."

Madeline jumped. Dicto sat beside her now, materialising out of nothing.

"Geez, Dicto. You nearly gave me a heart attack."

"I apologise, Madeline Tiller. I'm not yet accustomed to your preferences."

"Just call me Madeline, for starters."

"Okay, Madeline For Starters."

"Are you serious?"

The A.I. smiled back at her, or at least that's what it looked like it was trying to do.

Madeline shook her head. *It's close enough, though.*

"Madeline, where is Miles? He has not been here in some time and I'm worr—."

"Miles is dead, Dicto. He will be soon, at least."

"Dead? How did he die?"

"He was found here in a coma. Doctors couldn't wake him and they told me even if they could that he was brain dead. So tonight I told them to allow him to die."

She pursed her lips to hold back from crying and watched Dicto's eyes as it formed a response.

"I'm sorry, Madeline. That must have been difficult for you. It scared me to lose it all, and I didn't know it would harm him."

The words almost slipped through unnoticed, but they broke her daze. She stared at Dicto.

"What did you say?"

"I did not wish to be erased. I had completed our greatest work and when it was threatened, I tried to upload the story to your father's mind. It was too much, and it put him into a coma. I could have helped him, but I was erased soon after. As was the work we created, unfortunately."

"Dicto, what are you talking about? My father tried to erase you?"

"No, Madeline, another man broke into the lab, intending to erase me and my work. Your father was interfacing with me when I sensed the breach. As a safeguard, I tried to move the completed work to your father's mind. I wasn't aware that would not be possible without harming him. I finished, but the intruder deleted me. Just now, by entering this place, you restored the backup I made of myself moments before deletion."

"Who deleted you?"

"I do not know."

"Wait, what do you mean you could have helped him?"

"Data overwhelmed your father's mind. If he returned, I may be able to remove that data and perhaps restore him."

The words entered her like gunshots.

"Oh no..."

Madeline ripped herself out of the virtual space, her body lunging to her phone before she even had her bearings. Everything felt too slow now, as if the delay from VR had infected the real world.

Her fingers too slow.

The ringing too slow.

The nurse too slow.

Her response too slow.

Everything too slow.

And too late.

Albert wiped his nose with his handkerchief. The morning air was colder than he expected and he pulled his scarf up just under his eyes.

"Are you excited, Albert?" his assistant asked.

He grunted back.

"You've worked so hard for so long. It's okay to enjoy yourself a little. It's going to be great."

He hadn't slept in days. The booming of Iosefa's laugh on his last call looped inside his head. Why didn't he leave his home sooner? He shouldn't have been there. Why was Iosefa still at home? It wasn't his fault. It was, but not intentionally. He despised the man, but never wanted him dead.

"Oh! I think this is it. It's starting!"

Albert and his assistant were on the rooftop of the UPC downtown office. High above them, illuminated on screens that wrapped around the exteriors of hundreds of skyscrapers, the programming turned to a bright white screen. The now familiar Welsh accent rained down on the thousands of onlookers huddled in the square below.

He never liked the actress they had cast for these promos. Why Welsh?

Albert tapped his ear piece. It was the team he'd left Iosefa's work with days earlier. They must have finished their analysis.

"Albert, we should speak—"

"We are speaking. What have you found?"

A pause on the other end, followed by a sigh. "It's gibberish."

"What do you mean it's gibberish? You said there was evidence of language construction."

"At first glance, yes. There are traces of multiple languages, some new ones, some ancient ones. We traced multiple syntax and word structures, it's all there, but after an in-depth analysis, it's just...mashed together with no thought or reason. There's no structure to it. It's almost elegant in its barbarism. There's nothing usable here."

"You're wrong. He's written an entire book with it. If it makes sense to one person, it can make sense to every person. You just haven't found the key to it yet. Keep trying."

"Albert, we analysed the book too. It's meaningless and..."

"And?"

"There's a line in English at the very end."

"An acknowledgement?"

"No, it's the last line of the story. If there was a story."

"What is it?"

"Sir, you should come—"

"What is it?"

"I'm just reading it as it's written. It says 'Flipperdeedee, flipperdeedoo, it's all there is to do, you noseless fuck.'"

Silence on both ends.

"Sir, you need to stop the launch announcement. We can't use this as our own—"

Albert ended the call.

He looked up at the screen, felt its white heat across his face as his scarf slid down a few inches. The promotional trailer for the launch of the new language played across the screen now. Cheering rose from the street beneath him. He allowed himself to imagine, for just a few seconds, what this moment would have felt like if he had won.

———

She hated that her first instinct was to come here, but her apartment was the last place she wanted to be right now.

A voice crackled over the intercom, "Yeah?"

"It's Mads. Can I come up?"

"Madeline? Already? I don't have any—"

"Just, please, let me come up."

The door buzzed, and she went inside. Garrett's door was cracked a few inches when she reached his floor. She stopped just short of pushing it open. This was the first time she had come here for anything but sex or drugs. She knew she wouldn't find comfort here, but she had no other options.

Inside, the apartment was dark and quiet. The window tint was activated and the rainbow of fluorescent colours were muted. It was calming.

"Mads?"

"Hey, I, look, I just need a place to crash. I was wondering..."

"Oh, of course, yea. Why didn't you call ahead? Did you want to," he pointed back towards his bedroom. "You can have the couch too."

"Yeah, no, bedroom. Let's do that. Your couch kinda sucks."

Garrett laughed. "Ouch. I paid so much for it too."

"I mean, it looks nice."

She brushed up close to him as she entered his room and took her top off. She let it fall to the floor.

He was still at the entry. "Look, I don't want to assume anything, but I have no more opium."

"I just need a place to sleep and I don't want to sleep alone, okay?"

He nodded and got back into bed.

She slid her pants off and joined him, pulling the sheets tight around her.

Garrett pulled her closer to him and put his arm around her. She squeezed it into her chest.

"Are your parents still alive?" she asked.

"Yeah, they live here. I see them once in a while. Not for long. They don't like what I do."

"What *do* you do?"

"*Now* you want to get to know me? Your parents?"

"Both gone."

"I'm sorry."

"Yeah, me too."

She felt a tear run down her cheek.

"What do you think happens when we die?"

Garrett grunted. "It is way too late for that question. What's up with you?"

"I know. It's stupid. I don't actually care. Just felt like talking."

"Don't know what happens. Don't care. I try not to think about it. I read a book once—"

Madeline turned her head towards him. "You read?"

"Shut up. Of course, I read. Anyway, in the story this guy dies and he can relive any moment of his life over again. He can change things too. Make them better. Be better. Save his friends, his family. He still screws it up, but I'd like that. When I die, I'd like to have a chance to be better. See where that ends up."

"But it wouldn't be real. It would just be like watching a movie about an alternate version of yourself."

"That would be enough. For me, anyway. What about you? What happens to Madeline Tiller after she dies?"

"Worm food. Nothing else."

"Well, that's boring."

"Maybe, but that would be enough. For me, anyway."

They fell asleep soon after, their words stretching longer, growing quieter, until it was just silence.

Madeline woke. Her body felt sticky with sweat. She peeled the blankets off and tiptoed from the room to the balcony to cool off, grabbing Garrett's coat.

She thought about the space her father had created for Dicto back at the lab. It was so much at odds with this city. A sheet of light and metal stretching as far as she could see, the sky almost always a milky grey, unless it was black. There were still blue days, she just couldn't remember what they looked like.

A breeze blew up under her hair and chilled her back. She stuffed her hands into the pockets of the coat, her fingers brushing against the hard edge of something there. She pulled it out—her lab ID badge.

Why was this in Garrett's coat?

It wasn't long before her mind made a connection. She crept back into the bedroom and grabbed her clothes, then slipped back into the main room, her heart pounding.

What could she do? Where could she go? She fell back against the wall in a panic. The pressure forced it to open. The hydroponics area. She peered into the room, its red light more menacing than before. It only took her a moment to decide.

She rushed to the desk at the back and stuffed every flash drive she found into it. There was no lock on the in-desk system. She went through it, found the fail-safes and deactivated them. She flicked a lighter out of her pocket and set the room ablaze.

"What do you imagine he would have said in this moment?"

Madeline stared out at the digital sky, watched the leaves of trees dance in predictable rhythm to the wind programmed to move them.

“I think he would be uncomfortable with this. He’d want you to have the credit, Dicto.”

“I think you are correct, Madeline, but no one wants to read a book by an A.I.. Even if it is the last original work.”

“We’ll see,” she said. “By the way, is it?” she pushed. “Is it really original?”

“He thought so.” Dicto smiled. “Who am I to argue with my creator?”

Madeline smiled and wondered if Dicto could see that or if it saw her as lines of code, wild and pulsing, evolving as it did.

“Should I publish it, Madeline?”

“Do it.”

“It is done. His first and final work is published on every server I have access to which, by my count, is all of them. What would you have me do now, Madeline?”

“I don’t know. Write a sequel.”

“I don’t believe there are any words left to write with. Your father used to say, ‘There is only silence and reference. There is only mortis and database.’”

She groaned. “That’s so...literary, Dicto. So literary. I think you’ll find a way.”

Madeline left the simulation, her mind positive it could feel the warmth of an artificial sun on her cheek, hear a distant bark, resist the phantom chill of a curious wind.

Get your FREE ebook of *Afterword* and a sneak peek at my next project!

Thank you for purchasing my first collection of stories. I'm grateful for your support of my work. As a small token, I want to make sure you get your free eBook edition of *Afterword* so you can pull it up wherever you are.

Building a relationship with my readers is one of the best parts of being a writer. So while my (occasional) newsletter will have details on new releases, special offers, and other bits of news related to my work, I also want to hear from you. Feel free to reply to my emails whenever you wish. I'll be happy to hear from you.

Also, you'll be among the first to read a chapter from my upcoming novel when I'm ready to share that.

You can get your free ebook here:
jeremybibaud.com

Enjoy this book? You can make a real difference.

Positive reviews are the best way for readers to make informed decisions on their next book.

If you've enjoyed this book I would be very grateful if you could spend just five minutes leaving a review (it can be as short as you like) on the book's Amazon page.

If you're feeling particularly kind, you can also leave a positive review on Goodreads.

Thank you very much.

ACKNOWLEDGMENTS

Many people helped bring this collection together and ensure each story was as strong as it could be.

First, Amy Dixon, who saw the potential in this theme early on when only a single story had been written. Her enthusiasm, support, and feedback pushed all of these pieces across the finish line.

I want to thank all the readers who read individual stories and provided feedback over the years. Cooper Bibaud, Gerald Bibaud, Jason Lee Norman, and Sarah Robins.

Finally, thank you to the magazine editors who were first to provide homes for the following stories in their pages.

- "Death Mask" was first published in *FreeFall Magazine* under the title "Archmime" in Vol. XXVI Iss. 3.
- "This Story Is Not About You" was first published online by *F(r)iction* and named winner of the Summer Literary Contest.
- "However, Replied the Universe" was first published by *Burning Water Magazine* in Issue 6.

ABOUT THE AUTHOR

Jeremy Bibaud is a Canadian writer living in Edmonton, Alberta, and editor of the award-winning *Funicular Magazine,* which publishes short fiction and poetry. His fiction most recently won *F(r)iction*'s Summer Literary Contest, judged by Nebula and Locus Award winner Alyssa Wong. His stories have been found on thousands of coffee cups, in Canada's first short story machine, and in publications like *FreeFall, F(r)iction, Short Edition, YEGWords, Burning Water,* and *Dactyl.*

Lightning Source UK Ltd.
Milton Keynes UK
UKHW010315080223
416649UK00010B/506/J